The Life-Changing List

An emotional, uplifting new duet from
Scarlet Wilson and Kate Hardy

The lives of Darcy and Felicity Bennett have
been at a standstill since losing their
beloved sister Laura five years ago.

But Laura had suspected this would happen,
so she'd arranged for her solicitor to give them
both a bucket list to bring the sisters back
together and help them sort out their lives.

Join Darcy and Felicity as they take on the list—
and find two handsome companions to
help them find joy in life again!

Read Darcy's story in
Slow Dance with the Italian
by Scarlet Wilson

And read Felicity's story in
A Fake Bride's Guide to Forever
by Kate Hardy

Available now!

Dear Reader,

I've always wanted to write a bucket list book—and when I discovered that my friend Scarlet Wilson felt the same way, it was obvious that we should team up for a duet...

So we have the Bennett sisters—and, yes, you are going to cry from this, because they lose their middle sister. And she's the one who asks them to do a bucket list in her memory (via a letter through the family solicitor).

Felicity (Fizz), the youngest, is as effervescent as her nickname. She's always kept Oliver firmly in the best friend zone, but she sees him in a new light when they have a wild weekend in Paris. He's the one who helps her with her list. But when his father becomes ill and asks him to take over the business, somehow in the hospital his dad gets the wrong idea and thinks that Fizz and Oli went to Paris to get engaged. Fizz agrees to be Oli's fake fiancée until his dad's health improves—but then the truth comes out and it all gets terribly messy...

Can she go from being fake to forever?

Read on, dear reader, and find out!

Kate Hardy

A FAKE BRIDE'S GUIDE TO FOREVER

KATE HARDY

Harlequin

ROMANCE

Harlequin® ROMANCE

ISBN-13: 978-1-335-59675-8

A Fake Bride's Guide to Forever

Recycling programs for this product may not exist in your area.

Harlequin Enterprises ULC
22 Adelaide St. West, 41st Floor
Toronto, Ontario M5H 4E3, Canada
www.Harlequin.com

Printed in U.S.A.

Kate Hardy has always loved books and could read before she went to school. She discovered Harlequin books when she was twelve and decided that this was what she wanted to do. When she isn't writing, Kate enjoys reading, cinema, ballroom dancing and the gym. You can contact her via her website, katehardy.com.

Books by Kate Hardy

Harlequin Romance

Snowbound with the Brooding Billionaire
One Week in Venice with the CEO
Crowning His Secret Princess
Tempted by Her Fake Fiancé
Wedding Deal with Her Rival

Harlequin Medical Romance

Twin Docs' Perfect Match

Second Chance with Her Guarded GP
Baby Miracle for the ER Doc

Yorkshire Village Vets

Sparks Fly with the Single Dad

Surgeon's Second Chance in Florence
Saving Christmas for the ER Doc
An English Vet in Paris

Visit the Author Profile page
at Harlequin.com for more titles.

For Scarlet—always a joy to work with you! xxx

**Praise for
Kate Hardy**

"Ms. Hardy has written a very sweet novel about
forgiveness and breaking the molds we place
ourselves in...a good heartstring novel that will
have you embracing happiness in your heart."

—*Harlequin Junkie* on *Christmas Bride for the Boss*

CHAPTER ONE

FIZZ GLANCED AT her phone for the umpteenth time. All of twelve seconds had passed since she'd last checked, even though it felt more like several minutes.

Oliver was nearly twenty minutes late.

It wasn't like him: her best friend was the epitome of organised, taking everything in his stride with a smile on his face and never being late for anything. Had something awful happened? Her nerves, already taut from wondering just what her sister Laura had written in her last letter, stretched that little bit tighter.

Then she saw the heads turning, looked in the same direction and let out the breath she hadn't even realised she was holding as she saw him walking into the wine bar. Oliver Harrison was the archetypal tall, dark and handsome man. Add eyes as blue as a spring sky and a ready smile that reached his eyes, and it was no wonder that women turned to stare at him as he passed. He had the same kind of stage presence as a movie star or rock hero.

He lifted a hand to acknowledge her; she mirrored the gesture, noting the disappointment on several female faces around him as they realised that he was meeting someone. Two minutes later, he slid into the booth opposite her and replaced her empty glass with a glass of chilled white wine. 'I assumed you'd like your usual,' he said.

A crisp and fruity New Zealand Sauvignon Blanc: her favourite. 'Thank you. Is everything OK, Oli?' she asked, concerned about that look of strain in his eyes—or was she projecting her own anxieties onto him?

'Just something I needed to sort out in the office that took a bit longer than I expected,' he said. 'Sorry. I should've texted you so you didn't worry. I thought I could make the time up, but then there was a delay on the Tube.'

Oliver's loveliness wasn't only in his looks: he was kind, thoughtful and paid attention. Yet more reasons why Fizz valued him so much. Her best friend was the most important person in her life outside her sisters and her parents.

'I was a bit surprised you asked me to meet you tonight. I thought you'd be with your family after you'd seen the solicitor—or at least with Darcy,' he said.

Her oldest sister. The one who'd met the solicitor with her…and then left. Fizz lifted a shoulder with a casualness she didn't feel. 'Mum and Dad are in the south of France.' Not because they'd forgotten Laura's anniversary, but because they still couldn't bear it. They'd gone to Provence to put distance between themselves and their home in Bath where her other sister Laura had taken her last breath. 'And Darcy had to go back to Edinburgh. Work.'

It was five hours between London and Edinburgh by train, and seven and a half by car: of course Darcy had needed to leave straight after their quick cocktail in the bar next door to the solicitor's office. But Fizz had hoped that Darcy might stay a bit longer. Just long enough to open Laura's letters to them together, rather than tackling them alone. Especially as today was the fifth anniversary of Laura's death from leukaemia. She usually kept Laura's anniversary as a quiet day, missing her middle sister's sunny nature; but the day felt heavier than usual, today.

Darcy had suggested they could text each other about the letters, instead. Fizz didn't suggest a phone or video call because *she* wouldn't want to have that kind of conversation in the corridor of a train so she wasn't going to make Darcy do that. Faced with behaving like the needy, annoying little sister who demanded attention—and that wasn't who she wanted to be—Fizz had forced a smile she didn't feel and agreed that texting would be fine.

It seemed that the distance between herself and Darcy wasn't just physical any more; it was becoming emotional as well.

And that *really* hurt.

It was bad enough that the 'Trouble Trio', as their parents had always called them when they were tiny, were a duo now that Laura was gone. Did Darcy want them to become the Sad Singles? Or was she just overreacting on a day she always found difficult? Fizz didn't really trust her judgement where Laura was concerned. Or Darcy. All she knew was that she missed her sisters.

Both of them.

Oliver reached across the table and squeezed her hand briefly. 'Are you OK, Fizz?'

'Yes,' she fibbed.

He raised both eyebrows and stared at her. She caved. Of course he knew her well enough to realise that she wasn't OK. He'd been her best friend for seven years, since they'd met at a mutual friend's birthday party in her first year at art school while he'd been in the first term of doing his Master's in Arts and Cultural Management. They'd talked all night, to the point of grabbing a mug of coffee from the kitchen and going to the top of Primrose Hill to watch the sunrise together, and they'd never looked back.

'No, I'm not all right,' she admitted, and lifted her chin. 'But I will be.'

'What did the solicitor have to say?' Oliver asked.

Fizz drew the envelope from her bag. Even seeing Laura's familiar handwriting looping across it made her catch her breath. Laura had even sketched a tiny champagne bottle with the cork flying out and bubbles cascading everywhere. Felicity Bennett, the youngest of the three sisters, had been known to everyone as 'Fizz' ever since she'd pronounced her name that way as a toddler, and turned out to have an effervescent personality to match. 'Laura.' The name came out as a wobble.

'Take a gulp of wine, breathe, then tell me,' he said gently.

The wine didn't help. Neither did breathing. But the concern in Oliver's eyes did the trick. 'OK. Mr Cochrane—the solicitor—gave us a letter.' Fizz had been the one to read it aloud in the office, and the tears had slid down her face with every word. 'Laura was worried about us. Darcy and me.' She blinked back the tears, refusing to let them overwhelm her again. 'She left the solicitor something to give us today if we weren't settled…happy.'

Of course their clear-sighted middle sister would've worked out what was likely to happen and planned for it.

A few months before Laura's death, Darcy had been jilted at the altar and fled to Edinburgh. Fizz had been torn between going with her oldest sister, who she knew was heartbroken and needed someone to help her through it, and supporting her middle sister, who she knew was dying. Darcy had made the decision for her: Laura's next round of chemo was in two days' time, so in Darcy's view Laura was the one who needed the most support. Darcy had told Fizz to stay put and look after their sister.

So Fizz had stayed in Bath, and texted Darcy regularly to check she was OK.

Darcy had returned five days later, her head clear and knowing what she wanted to do next. And she'd stayed in Bath in the dark days when they knew Laura was dying. Fizz had rearranged a couple of her classes so she could spend long weekends at home, and she and Darcy had taken it in turns with their mum and dad to look after Laura, bringing their sister little treats to make her smile and making sure she got to see everyone she wanted to say goodbye to, in between resting.

After Laura's funeral, Darcy had gone back to Edinburgh. Damian had broken her trust, and since then she hadn't dated much, if at all. She worked too hard; although her immaculate make-up could hide the shadows under her eyes, it couldn't hide the ones in them. Fizz didn't even know where to start dealing with those shadows. Not when Darcy refused to let her help and claimed that she was absolutely fine.

Fizz herself had gone back to art college in London. And she hadn't told a soul about the day after Laura's death. She'd gone back to London briefly to see her tutors and arrange a couple of weeks of compassionate leave from her course, plus pick up her sketchbook and the project she'd been working on as part of her second-year degree assessment. That night, something had happened. She'd kept it locked away in a box ever since and buried it as deep in her heart as she could. It was the reason why she never let a relationship go past the third date, any more.

Shame burned through her. What would Darcy say, if she knew? What would Laura have said?

But Fizz would never tell her secret. Not to anyone. Not even Oliver, who'd been in New York when it happened.

Oliver, who'd just asked her what the solicitor had said. If she didn't tell him something, and fast, he'd start asking questions that she might not want to answer. 'She left us a task. And some money.'

'What type of task?'

'It's a bucket list.' The words from the letter she'd read out loud in the solicitor's office, holding Darcy's hand, were practically engraved on her heart. 'She said, "I want to push you both to maybe do something you haven't. I want my sisters to have fun. Have fun in my memory. Know that I am right by your side when you do all these things. I love you girls.'"

Typical Laura. She'd always been the sunniest of the three sisters; and it was because of Laura that Fizz's signature jewellery range was based on sunflowers. Not just because they'd been Laura's favourite flowers; Fizz saw her work as something to brighten someone's day, just as Laura had always brightened everyone's day around her. Of course Laura would always be there with them both, in spirit—and she'd be there with them as they carried out her bucket list.

'A bucket list where you have fun is a really nice way to celebrate someone as special as your sister,' Oliver said. 'I assume you and Darcy are doing it together?'

'Apparently we're supposed to do it on our own.' Maybe that was why Darcy had wanted to open the envelopes separately. Fizz lifted one shoulder in another shrug that she hoped looked casual. 'We might not even have the same list.'

He frowned. 'Don't you know that already?'

'I haven't opened mine yet.'

His frown deepened. 'Why didn't you and Darcy open the envelopes together?'

'Darcy thought it'd be better to wait and do

it separately.' Fizz aimed for toneless, but of course Oliver knew her too well. He'd know exactly how much that stung.

'And the meeting was this morning?' he asked.

'Lunchtime. Darcy caught the first train from Edinburgh this morning. I met her at King's Cross.' And she'd tried not to feel hurt that Darcy hadn't wanted to spend the whole of today with her. Her sister had a demanding job; and they both dealt with things in different ways. Darcy buried herself in work, and Fizz… Fizz had spent the rest of the day walking, lost in her memories and trying not to let the sadness overwhelm her.

Clearly guessing what was in her head, Oliver reached over to squeeze her hand briefly. 'You could open the envelope with me, if you like?'

She nodded, not trusting the lump in her throat to let the words out and knowing he'd realise how grateful she was for that offer.

She turned the envelope over, slid her little finger into the gap where the flap of the envelope wasn't stuck to the back, and eased the flap open. Then she took out the folded piece of paper and placed it on the table between herself and Oliver, so they both had to turn slightly to read it.

'"Fizz's bucket list,"' she read. Laura had doodled a bucket containing an uncorked bottle of champagne, with little bubbles popping out of the top.

Oliver smiled and gestured to the doodle. 'That's lovely. I can almost see her sketching that.'

'It feels like a hug,' Fizz admitted. 'She must've doodled something on Darcy's, too.' But so far her oldest sister hadn't shared much: just that Laura had left little personal messages all over the bucket list.

'"It's up to you how you do this,"' Fizz read, returning to the letter. '"On your own, or with someone else. And it's up to you what order you do them in. Just do them within six weeks. Most of all, have fun. Love you, L."'

'Six weeks. Four items—that works out at one every ten days or so, which is doable,' Oliver said. 'Unless she's asking you to climb a mountain or run a marathon, in which case you need to train properly first.'

'She wouldn't ask me to climb a mountain. She knows I'd worry about damaging my hands and not being able to work,' Fizz said.

She glanced back at the list. Each item was written in capitals and bullet-pointed with a sunflower.

Do something that scares you.

Fizz blew out a breath. 'Laura said she wanted to push me. She wasn't kidding: the first one is to do something that scares me. But, hey, nothing scares me.' Well. One thing did. But she'd never admit that to a living soul, not even Oliver—because then she'd have to follow through. And she wanted to keep that bit of her life buried. 'Something that scares me,' she mused. 'What exactly do I do with that?'

The one thing Oliver was pretty sure his best friend was scared of was losing her other sister. But, given that Darcy hadn't stayed for long in London after the meeting with the solicitor, that was a bit too close to the bone right now. Saying it out loud and ripping open her wounds wasn't going to help, and it certainly wouldn't persuade Fizz to talk. With his best friend, he'd learned to take the oblique approach. She was always full of smiles, but since Laura's death she'd used that smile as a shield, not letting anyone see what was really in her heart. Even he got the super-glittery smile from her, from time to time.

Instead of pushing her, he suggested, 'You could start with people's most common fears. Did you know the top three in the UK are heights, spiders, and small spaces?'

He could see the relief in Fizz's eyes that he wasn't going to put any pressure on her to talk, right now, and knew he'd done the right thing.

'How do you know that?' she demanded.

'It was in an article I read last week on an in-flight magazine.' He smiled. 'Which probably isn't *quite* the most tactful place to bring up a fear of small spaces.'

'I'm fine with heights and spiders,' Fizz said. 'And I'm not scared of small spaces.' She looked at him, her blue eyes narrowing, clearly not willing to admit what really scared her. 'You're right—other people's fears could be a good place to start. Can you remember anything else from that article?'

'Public speaking and clowns, I think. Hang on. I'll see if I can find it.' He took his phone from his pocket and tapped into a search engine. Within a few seconds, he'd found the article. 'Here we go. Oh, you'll love this one.

How about pteromerhanophobia?' Teasing Fizz might give her the chance to ground herself and feel less vulnerable. The alternative was wrapping his arms round her and telling her he'd fight every single dragon for her: single-handedly, without a scrap of armour and while walking barefoot over a path of molten lava. But he didn't think she was ready to hear that. Not right now, and maybe not ever. So he'd keep it light, the way he always did.

'Obviously the last bit means "fear of",' she said, 'but the first?'

'Think of something that starts with "ptero",' he said.

'Pterodactyl,' she said promptly.

'Strictly speaking, that should be ptero-*saur*,' he said.

She rolled her eyes. 'You're *such* a pedant, Oliver Harrison.'

'It goes with my job, as well as yours. Attention to detail is important,' he retorted. If she was insulting him, that meant she wasn't going to cry. Which was a good thing. 'And a pterosaur is?'

'A flying dinosaur. OK. Fear of flying. Though you of course had to find the long word for it.'

She smiled at him, and his heart rate kicked

up a notch. Oliver just hoped it didn't show in his expression. He knew Fizz saw him as her best friend, not as a potential life partner. Definitely not as a lover. Apart from that moment when she'd told him about her middle sister's prognosis and he'd wrapped his arms round her, wanting to comfort her, and somehow they'd ended up sharing a kiss: a kiss that had melted his bones and made him want so much more. But he'd pulled back, knowing that Fizz was vulnerable and refusing to take advantage of that. He'd wanted her; but he wanted her to want him for *himself*, not for comfort. Back then he'd decided until Fizz was ready to give her heart to him, he wasn't going to tell her how he felt about her. But she never had. So he'd buried those feelings, determined to protect their friendship. She didn't need the pressure. But she did need him—as a friend. And if she thought he was a workaholic: well, that was a good enough cover for why he didn't date much. For now, anyway.

She steepled her fingers. 'What else are people scared of?'

'There's a new kid on the block: nomophobia. That's the fear of not having a mobile phone,' he said.

'Utterly ridiculous,' she said, dismissing it with a roll of her eyes. 'You can always borrow a phone from someone if your battery dies. And our parents and grandparents managed just fine without a mobile phone when they were our age. Any more?'

'Dentists, needles, dogs, balloons...oh, wait, here's one for you. Garlic.'

To his relief, this time she laughed. 'I love garlic dough balls. I'm not scared of garlic—or vampires, if that's what you were implying.' She raised her eyebrow at him. 'What are you scared of?'

I used to be afraid that you'd never fall in love with me, the way I fell in love with you.

He definitely wasn't sharing that one. 'Making a monumental cock-up at work when I'm valuing a painting—or losing my head at an auction and going way beyond Dad's maximum bid.'

She laughed. 'That's never going to happen. Not with your attention to detail.' She wrinkled her nose. 'And that wouldn't happen for me, either. I always check with my clients if I can't find the perfect stone within their budget, to see whether they'd be prepared to compromise on colour, clarity or size instead. I should've been working on a commission, this afternoon, but wrapping silver around really fragile gems isn't a good idea on a day when you can't concentrate properly. I didn't want to end up with a pile of fragments, so I'll catch up with myself tomorrow.' She shrugged. 'Better doing a super-long day than ruining my stock and having to start all over again.'

'What did you do after Darcy left?' he asked.

'A bit of urban hiking,' she said. 'I went to Primrose Hill.'

Where they'd watched the sunrise together, the first day they'd met. Had she gone there because it was a happy place for her, filled with good memories? He hoped so.

'I stopped for coffee, a couple of times. And I stuffed my face with cake, to the point where I definitely don't want dinner tonight.' She rolled her eyes. 'And, yes, I know cake isn't great nutrition.'

'Some days you just need cake. Tomorrow you can make up for it with a wheatgrass smoothie,' he said with a smile.

She grimaced. 'That's the worst thing I've ever tasted! I'll pass on the smoothie, but I promise I'll eat proper food tomorrow.' She paused. 'Something I'm scared of needs a bit more thought. I'll put that at the end of the list.' She looked at the paper in front of them. *"'Go somewhere nice and quiet, take time to reflect on what you want out of life.'"* She wrinkled her nose. 'That probably needs to be a later task, too.'

'How would you define "nice and quiet"?' he asked.

'A beach,' she said instantly. 'Not a tropical one—I want a big, wide, sandy one where you can watch the sun rise. Where the sea swishes on the shore.'

He wasn't surprised. Fizz was a sunrise rather than a sunset person. 'The east coast of England, then. Norfolk or Northumbria?'

'Or a garden. The sort you get at a stately home, but when it's not open. Something stuffed with colour and scent and loveliness.' She smiled. 'You know me and flowers.'

'Half the time, you're thinking about what kind of jewellery they put in your mind,' he said.

'Are you calling me a workaholic?' she asked. 'Because it takes one to know one.'

'I know.' A garden not open to the public, he could definitely offer her. But he wouldn't push her just yet. She needed time to work out what she wanted. 'What's next?'

"'Make a commitment to someone or something.'"

That would make her run a mile, Oliver knew. Apart from her career, Darcy and her parents—and himself, in terms of being her best friend—Fizz was very careful not to commit to anything or anyone. She'd practically stopped dating ever since Laura's death.

'She's added a note,' Fizz said. 'She says it has to be something that lasts a few years.'

'So, what? Do a qualification? Join some kind of club?'

Or commit to someone...

Oliver thought about the news he'd received before coming here. He needed to make a commitment himself. But he couldn't ask Fizz to do that with him. Not without risking losing the relationship he valued most, and he wasn't prepared to do that.

'I don't know.' She sighed. 'There's another note here to say it has to be something important.'

'Mentor someone?' he suggested.

She shrugged. 'Maybe. I think the easiest one is going to be the last one. *"Have a wild twenty-four hours in a European city you've always wanted to go to."* And apparently I can take someone with me.'

'Darcy?' he asked.

She shook her head. 'I don't think that's an option.'

He frowned. 'Surely Laura suggested it to help the two of you get close again?'

'Darcy's theory,' Fizz said, 'is that Laura wanted us to work things out for ourselves instead of leaning on each other.' She sighed. 'I have no idea which order to do them in. Do I do the easiest task first—or leave it until last, as a kind of reward?'

'What do you really want, Fizz?' he asked gently.

'A magic wand and a time-travelling device,' she said promptly. 'Neither of which exist.'

'Maybe they do—only not in the form you expect. Maybe this is both,' he said, indicating Laura's bucket list. 'A way of getting you to a place where it's easier to deal with things.'

'Maybe.' She gave him a tight smile. 'How do you fancy going to Paris, Oli?'

'I thought it was supposed to be somewhere you've always wanted to go to?' He looked at her, surprised. 'Wait a second—are you *seriously* telling me you've never been to Paris?'

'I've been to France, skiing and seeing the sunflower fields in Provence. But never the capital,' she confirmed.

'You went to art school for three years. *How* have you never visited Paris?' he asked.

'Because I went to Florence, Amsterdam and Vienna instead,' she said. 'With Paris being only a couple of hours from London by train, I thought it was somewhere I could go at any time.'

'But you've always been too busy?'

'Building a business means putting the hours in,' she said. 'And don't nag me. You work silly hours, too.'

For his dad's business.

Where everything was about to change. Not that he was planning to talk about that. Today, Laura's anniversary, was a day when Fizz needed him to support her, not lean on her. 'Uh-huh,' he said.

'You haven't answered the question, Oli. Will you come with me?'

Go with her to Paris. One of the most romantic cities in the world. The city of light, of wide boulevards and pretty little parks, of cafés where you could watch the world go by as you enjoyed amazing pastries. Paris in the spring, at its most romantic, full of blossom and wisteria and lovers strolling with their arms wrapped round each other.

It was probably the worst place he could

go to with Fizz. Yes, he'd forced himself to move on; but that involved protecting himself from further hurt, pain that would surely be caused by dancing with her on the banks of the Seine, or kissing her at the top of the Eiffel Tower! And yet, how was he supposed to resist doing those things in Paris? It was the City of Love!

On the other hand, right now she wasn't in a place where he could turn her down, even if he did it gently.

'Sure,' he said. 'When did you have in mind?'

'When do you have a space in your diary?'

He could move meetings easily enough. For her. He spread his hands. 'Whenever.'

'Let's go on Friday.'

'*This* Friday?' he asked, shocked.

'You did just say you could go at any time. Why wait?' She gave him her trademark impulsive smile, and his heart—annoyingly—did a backflip.

'All right. I'll book us somewhere,' he said. Somewhere to make her first trip to Paris special. He knew a gorgeous hotel just off the Champs-Élysées, with tall windows, elegant awnings, pretty wrought-iron balconies and a stunning Art Deco interior. She'd love it. And he knew some excellent restaurants, too. Fizz loved good food with good presentation. He could make sure she'd always remember her first time in Paris. *With him.*

'No,' she said. 'This is all part of the bucket list stuff, so it's on me.' She grinned. 'Which means I'm afraid it's not going to be whatever Paris's equivalent is of Kensington or Knightsbridge.'

He winced. 'I'm not *that* much of a snob.' Though Oliver's background had attracted a few women who were more interested in his bank balance than they were in him; he'd learned to spot the type early and avoid them.

'You're not any sort of snob. I was teasing.' She patted his arm. 'What I'm saying is, don't expect something swanky. It's going to be wild and impulsive.'

Which was her all over, he thought.

'Cheap, cheerful and *very* Parisian,' she continued. 'And we'll go by Eurostar.'

'More eco than a plane,' he said, approvingly, 'and a lot more convenient for getting to wherever we stay in the city.'

'Great. I'll book something tonight and text you the details,' she said.

He nodded his agreement. 'Is there anything in particular you want to see in Paris?'

'The Musée d'Orsay, and I know it'll be a

good idea to book tickets for that before we go,' she said. 'But the idea is to have a good time for twenty-four hours. Unplanned. Apart from seeing the clock and the Van Goghs at the gallery, we can go wherever the mood takes us.'

Oliver would rather plan the whole thing in advance, especially if they were limited to only twenty-four hours; without planning, how could they possibly fit in the gorgeous buildings of the Marais, the art at Montmartre, the narrow streets of the Latin Quarter, the Louvre and the Eiffel Tower? And he'd much rather buy skip-the-line tickets than waste half their time in Paris stuck in a queue.

But this was Fizz's list, so they needed to do it her way, not his. 'OK,' he said.

'So now it's your turn to spill,' she said. 'Tell me what's really wrong.'

'Nothing,' he said quickly. Too quickly, because she raised her eyebrows at him, and he caved just as fast as she had. 'Dad had a hospital appointment, this morning. I think it scared him.'

She reached across the table and squeezed his hand, letting him know that she was on his side no matter what.

At her touch, all Oliver's good intentions

of not leaning on her went straight out of the window. 'It scared him to the point where he's decided it's time to retire.' He took a deep breath. 'And he wants me to take over. To be the managing director of Harrison's Fine Art.'

'That's a good thing all round, isn't it?' she asked.

Yes—and no. He didn't know where to start with that one.

'You love your job, and you'll be the third generation of Harrisons to run the company. Plus it means your dad will take life a bit easier, so you won't have to worry about him quite so much,' Fizz said. 'OK, so you're only twenty-eight, and that's pretty young to take over a family business: but he's been training you for the role practically since you were a toddler. You've worked at the gallery since you were fifteen and you've spent the last six years doing a stint in every single part of the business. You know the business inside out; you've done everything from restoration and conservation through to curating exhibitions, preparing catalogues and dealing with artists and auctions.'

If it was only that, Oliver would be fine about it. He knew there wouldn't be any mut-terings at the gallery about the boss's son taking over, because everyone was well aware that he put in the hours, he listened to other people's ideas and he wouldn't ask anyone to do anything he wasn't prepared to do himself. He'd earned the job.

It was the rest of his dad's requirements that bothered him.

Now Fizz knew there was something wrong. Oliver wasn't paying attention. But it wasn't a dream that was distracting him; from the expression in his eyes, it was a nightmare. 'Oli?'

He gave her a bright smile that didn't reach his eyes at all. 'I'm fine.'

No, he wasn't. 'Just because today is—well, what it is,' she said, 'it doesn't mean you can't talk to me.' At the sceptical look on his face, she added, 'Think of it this way: telling me what's wrong will distract me and help me stop brooding about how much I miss Laura. It's always easier to fix someone else's problems than it is your own. Tell me what's wrong, and we both win.'

He grimaced. 'There are…' He looked as if he was trying to find the right word. 'Strings,' he finished lamely.

'What sort of strings?'

He took a deep breath. 'Dad wants me to get married and have kids.'

'And that's a condition of you getting the job?' She winced. 'Oli, that's really not fair. Not to mention going against just about every bit of employment law there is. He wouldn't be able to make that demand of anybody else.'

'I know,' he said. 'But I'm not anybody else, am I? I'm his only child.'

'Surely he realises that it's better for you to marry someone because you want to spend the rest of your life with them, not because you want to please him?' Fizz asked. 'It's not OK to tell someone else to have kids for your sake, either. What if it turns out that you or your future wife can't have kids?' She frowned. 'I know you said he had a hospital appointment today that shook him up a bit, but what he wants from you is completely unreasonable.'

'I know,' Oliver acknowledged. 'But it's not because he's a control freak. It's because he's scared. He wants to see me settled before he dies.'

The worry in his eyes flickered again, and she realised what Oliver wasn't saying. That he thought he was going to lose his dad much, much earlier than he'd ever expected. And she knew how bad it felt, to watch someone you loved die and not be able to do a thing to save them. She'd been there herself, five years ago. 'Sorry. Ignore what I just said. If he's that sick, of course it changes things.' She bit her lip. 'And you know I'll support you. Is it…?' She caught her breath. She couldn't face using *that* word today, but she knew Oliver would understand what she meant. And she'd be there for him.

'No. It's not what Laura had,' Oliver said gently. 'It's his heart. Apparently it's developed an abnormal rhythm. Considering he doesn't eat meat, he drinks decaf coffee and he has no more than one glass of red wine a day, he's pretty upset,' he added. 'Dad thought he was doing everything right to keep himself healthy.'

'You haven't mentioned exercise,' she said. 'Sitting at your desk is meant to be the killer.'

'That's what really shocked him—suddenly being out of breath on a short walk, as if he'd been running up a hill instead of strolling through the park. He's scared of taking Poppy out for a walk now, in case he collapses and drops the lead and she ends up in the road and gets run over.' He grimaced. 'Which I know is catastrophising, but he can't see past the fear.'

'When did it all happen?' she asked.

'It started a couple of months ago. He's been keeping it from me because he didn't want to make a fuss over nothing, but he admitted he saw the GP. The doctor gave him some medication, but it hasn't made Dad's heart rate normal again so the GP referred him. And he's tired all the time. As of this morning, the specialist was talking about surgery.' He took a deep breath. 'Dad's really, really scared he'll die before he gets the chance to see me settle down and have a family of my own.'

And she'd just told him his dad was being unreasonable.

Mark Harrison wasn't trying to be a control freak and organise his son's life, the way she'd assumed; instead, he was scared that he wouldn't see his beloved only child settle down with someone who'd make him happy and feel supported for the rest of his life. Hadn't Laura worried about precisely the same thing where Fizz and Darcy were concerned? She'd given the instructions to the solicitor.

'Considering my sister sent me a message from the grave for a very similar reason,' Fizz said, 'I should probably take back most of what I said. Though I do think your dad's gone a bit too far. Laura didn't say I had to get married and have kids. She just wanted me to...' She paused, trying to think how to put it. 'Stop grieving so much and start living, I suppose.'

'She could probably have written that bucket list for me,' Oliver said. 'Do something that scares me—that'd be taking over Harrison's Fine Art, because I didn't think I'd be doing that for at least another five years, and what if I mess it up?'

'Of course you won't. You're way too organised and capable to do that,' she said.

'Thank you.' He blew out a breath. 'And I have to make a commitment.'

'To the firm, yes; but you don't have to make the commitment your dad wants you to make, to someone else,' she said. 'That's where I think one of the other things on the list comes in. You need to find a quiet place to think and reflect on what *you* want from life, Oli. If that's the same as what your dad wants, then go right ahead. If it isn't, then don't get married to the first suitable woman you find, because you'll just make yourself miserable—not to mention your bride. And then your dad will feel guilty that he's ruined your life and it'll affect his health. It's a vicious circle.' She lifted a shoulder. 'You can come in with my beach-or-garden reflection trip, if you want.'

'I might just take you up on that,' he said. 'I'm happy to drive us both, any time you choose. And maybe your twenty-four hours of fun in Paris will help me chill out enough to come to terms with the rest of it.'

'Good. Given what you've just told me, are you really sure you can fit in going to Paris this week?'

He gave her a wry smile. 'I'm sure.'

'Then I'll book everything and let you know what time you need to be at St Pancras on Friday morning.' She squeezed his hand again. 'I'm sorry your dad's ill, Oli. I'm here whenever you need me. If you want to talk at three in the morning, that's fine. Just call me. And if I can do anything to help—drop in and distract him, and challenge him to a game of chess or something, just let me know.'

'Thank you. And I hope you know I'm here for you,' he said, raising his own glass. 'To us. And to Laura's bucket list.'

'To us,' she echoed. 'And to Laura's bucket list.'

* * *

Later that evening, Fizz adopted the nearest she could get to a yoga lotus pose in the middle of her living room, and thought about what Oliver had told her.

Married, with children.

That would change everything between them. They wouldn't be able to spend as much time together as they did now; of course his partner would want him to spend more of his time with her and their children.

And it really should've occurred to her before now that Oliver would settle down with someone, one day. Just because she'd learned the hard way that love ruined things—she'd never forget how her sister Darcy's heart had been broken by Damian jilting her, and how deep the hurt had gone—and Oliver had fended off more than his fair share of gold-diggers in the past, it didn't mean that he wouldn't want to try and find love in the future.

Though, now she thought about it, he didn't actually date very much. She could probably count the number of women he'd dated during the last couple of years on the fingers of one hand. And none of his relationships had lasted very long, either. She'd assumed that it was because Oliver had been focused on making sure he knew every part of his family's business, knowing that one day he'd be taking it over, and his girlfriends hadn't been prepared to wait for him.

Though the timescale on Oliver taking over Harrison's Fine Art seemed to have changed from 'sometime' to 'right now', in the space of two seconds. And if he was serious about finding a bride…

It suddenly felt as if someone had strapped her into a G-force simulation rig and turned the velocity up to full.

She blew out a breath. Maybe Paris would be the last real time she and Oliver would spend together. Who was it who'd said about them always having Paris? It was a film, she was sure; Laura the film buff would've known, but she couldn't ask Laura any more.

Fizz unpeeled herself from the not-quite-there lotus pose, grabbed her laptop and flicked into the internet to check it out. Of course. Bogart to Bergman, in *Casablanca*. Not that her situation or Oliver's had anything in common with the movie.

Paris. A wild twenty-four hours they'd always have to look back on.

They'd have fun. Eat flaky croissants and

glossy *macarons*, baguettes and good cheese. People-watch while they sipped espressos or red wine. Maybe they'd hop on a bus or a boat to see some of the famous sights, then lose themselves in the narrow back streets to find a different side of the city.

'Yeah. We'll always have Paris,' she said, and started looking for an apartment to stay in.

CHAPTER TWO

ON FRIDAY MORNING, eyes gritty from lack of sleep and half wishing he'd never agreed to this, Oliver met Fizz at the Eurostar check-in.

'Five minutes past six. I mean, I know you're all about the sunrise instead of the sunset, but this is a completely uncivilised time of the morning,' he grumbled.

She handed him a bamboo cup with a silicone lid and rolled her eyes at him. 'Don't say another word to me, Oliver Harrison, until you've drunk at least half of this. Our train's at seven, which means we'll be in Paris at twenty past nine. We'll drop off our stuff, and then we get to explore the City of Light for twenty-four glorious hours.'

'We'll hardly scratch the surface in twen—'

'Shh.' She pressed one fingertip against his lips, and his entire body felt as if it were tingling. 'No more talking until the caffeine's kicked in.' She grinned. 'I bet at work they've learned to greet you with coffee at the door.'

'I'm not that bad,' he muttered.

'Yes, you are. Being a night owl, you're only reasonable at this time of the morning if you've stayed up.'

He could happily work until two in the morning, whereas Fizz normally fell asleep before half-past ten. Oliver was never sure how she'd managed to come by her reputation as a party girl. Maybe it was because she usually found a way to snatch some sleep in the middle of a party and then be awake again at four in the morning, fresh as a daisy. Though she'd stay up all night if it meant catching a meteor shower or a lunar eclipse. Just as he'd drag himself out of bed at a ridiculous hour to watch the sunrise with her.

'Come on. Let's check in and find our seats. And I've already sorted breakfast, before you ask. We have carbs.' She held up a large paper bag bearing the logo of one of the shops on the concourse.

This was the Fizz he was used to. Irrepressibly cheerful, full of smiles and bright ideas, rather than the woman he'd met in a bar earlier this week, on the edge of tears. He knew that Fizz and her sisters had their own tagline—*We're the Bennett sisters: we can do anything*—and usually she lived up to it.

Today she was wearing jeans and canvas shoes, teamed with a bright flowery shirt, a pair of dark glasses and a straw sunhat; she looked incredibly pretty. He was glad he'd asked her what the dress code was for their trip, because he too was wearing jeans, a light shirt and canvas shoes—a far cry from the beautifully cut suit and handmade Italian shoes he'd normally wear at the gallery on a Friday morning. Her backpack was small; he knew she'd learned the art of travelling light a long time ago. His own luggage was equally minimal, for the same reason; he'd rather spend his time doing something than queuing for baggage.

Once they were settled in their seats, she unpacked the contents of the paper bag. 'Warm brioche bun filled with brie, bacon and cranberry—there are two for you; *pain au chocolat*, also warm; a punnet of raspberries; and freshly squeezed orange juice.' She looked gleeful. 'I was first in the queue. That's how I managed to pick up this lot *and* the coffee before I met you.'

'I hate to think what time you arrived here.'

The coffee was just starting to unscramble his brain cells.

'Probably about the time you might consider going to bed. Eat,' she said. 'And then I'll tell you the sort-of schedule.' Her blue eyes sparkled with excitement. 'I can't wait to explore Paris with you.'

Was she excited about Paris, or about exploring it with *him*? Though he wasn't going to ask; until he was fully awake, the words would come out garbled—or, worse still, reveal things he'd buried long ago, which would be a complete disaster. Instead, he did what she'd suggested, and worked his way through the breakfast she'd bought them. A few minutes later, the carbs had done their work and he felt human again.

'Thank you,' he said. 'That was the perfect breakfast.'

'De rien, mon nounours,' she said with a smile.

'Your *what*?'

'Nounours. It means "teddy bear".' She sang a couple of lines of Elvis at him, swapping *'nounours'* for 'teddy bear'.

He couldn't help laughing. 'I hate to think what website you picked that up from.'

'Oh, it was a good one.' Her grin widened. *'Mon petit nounours en sucre.'*

'I'm not even going to try topping that one. Unless,' he said, 'you're *ma petite minette en sucre avec une cerise sur le dessus.'*

He waited while she worked it out, enjoying that little pleat just above her nose when she was concentrating, followed by the infectious laugh when she'd finished. 'Double pun—topped it with a topping. OK. You win. And your reward is...'

A kiss?

He pushed the thought back. Where was this even coming from? He'd put away those feelings years ago. Maybe it was everything with his father, the idea that marriage was so much closer than he'd planned, and that Fizz, for the first time in a long time, was being vulnerable with him again? Besides, that wasn't what the wild twenty-four hours was about.

'...finding me a seriously good *macaron*. A violet one.'

'I can do that,' he said, and went hot all over at the idea of lounging on the grass of a Parisian park with her, making her reach up to take a bite of *macaron*. He really needed to stop daydreaming! To give him breathing space to get his wayward thoughts back in control, he asked, 'So is there a plan?'

'Of course there's a plan. Actually, I'm bending Laura's rules a little bit, because I got this fabulous deal on an apartment in the north of the city—they'd had a very last-minute cancellation—so we're actually staying for two nights.'

'Two nights is good,' he said. 'Though I wish you'd told me, because then I could've booked somewhere for dinner tomorrow night.'

'That's precisely why I didn't tell you. This is my bill,' she reminded him. 'We're going for "cheap and cheerful" and having *fun*. We don't have to worry about dress codes or anything else. I booked tickets for the Musée d'Orsay this afternoon, but the rest of the time we're just going to wing it. I arranged with Eloise, the owner of the apartment, that I could drop our bags as soon as we arrive in Paris, so we're not going to waste a single second.'

'You don't want to think about which sights you'd like to see while we're on the train, and plot them on a map so we concentrate on one area at a time—rather than zig-zag all over the place and use up half our time in Paris on the Métro?' he checked.

'I know that's how you'd do it, but no.' She gave him an over-the-top wink. 'We have rules to follow. Laura wanted me to have a wild twenty-four hours, which means no real plans.'

'You're already breaking her rules by making it two nights instead of twenty-four hours,' he pointed out.

'Nope. That's merely a bit of creative interpretation. My sisters would both expect me to take advantage of a good deal,' she shot back.

He loved bickering with Fizz. She had an answer for everything.

'But, since you clearly want to sort-of plan things…where would a dealer in fine art and a jewellery designer *possibly* want to visit in Paris, apart from the Musée d'Orsay?' she asked, her blue eyes sparkling.

'You tell me.' He batted it back to her.

'I suppose it ought to be the Louvre and Montmartre,' she said. 'And the flea market—actually, as that's near our apartment, I thought we could do that one first thing tomorrow morning. I'll put an alarm on my phone so I don't drag you about all day rummaging for bargains.'

'Sounds good.' Relentless shopping definitely wasn't his idea of fun, and he was pretty sure it wasn't hers, either. 'What about the Eiffel Tower?' he asked.

'Absolutely.' She grinned. 'I want to do all of the touristy things—you know, pose as if I'm holding the Eiffel Tower in the palm of my hand, and dangling the Louvre pyramid from my finger and thumb.'

'I know just the spots where you can do that, and I'll take the photos for you,' he promised.

'What do you want to do?'

He shook his head. 'This is your trip. Your first time in Paris. So it's what *you* want to see that matters.'

'You've been to Paris before. What's your favourite thing?' she asked.

'The clock in the Musée d'Orsay,' he said. 'Which is touristy—so I'd say you need to take a photo there—but it's gorgeous and I like the art there more than anywhere else. And I like the Marais. It'd be fun to *flâner* there, even if it's only for a little while.'

'*Flâner?*' she asked, looking slightly confused.

'Wander around and people-watch,' he explained. 'Drink good coffee. Maybe persuade someone to let us look through one of the archways into the courtyards that aren't really open to the public.'

She beamed. 'I'm definitely up for that. And this is spring, so I want to see all the flowers.'

'The cherry blossom will be near the Eiffel Tower and in the gardens near the Louvre—the Tuileries and the Palais Royale. You might even get the end of the magnolias, and the beginnings of the wisteria and the roses as well,' he said.

'Wisteria. Hmm. That'd make interesting jewellery,' she said thoughtfully. 'Glass, enamel and seed beads. Definitely earrings; maybe even a necklace and bracelet set.'

'Hang on—do Laura's rules allow you to work while you're having a wild twenty-four hours in Paris?' he asked.

'I'm not actually *working*, just thinking,' she said. 'Just like you'll be doing in Montmartre.'

He was more likely to find the kind of art that his family's gallery dealt with in the Marais than in Montmartre, though he wasn't going to be snooty about it and make her feel bad. 'If you want to do classic touristy things, you need to have your portrait sketched in charcoal at Montmartre,' he said instead.

'Only if you have yours done as well,' she said. 'Actually, better than that, we should have a joint portrait.'

As friends, he reminded himself. 'Sure.'

The rest of the journey to the Gare du Nord whizzed by. Once they were through to the Métro, Oliver wasn't surprised to find that Fizz had their destination saved in the map on her phone. Although she was way more spontaneous than he was, he knew she wanted to make the most of their time in Paris, so she would've worked out how to get to their apartment from the train station, as well as how long it would take to get from the apartment to the city centre.

Once they left the underground, they emerged onto a busy Parisian street under a bright blue spring sky, then after a two-minute walk she led him through an archway that opened into a paved courtyard with buildings curved round it. The three-storey white townhouses had grey slate roofs, tall narrow windows and wrought-iron balconies; there were zinc tubs and huge terracotta pots bursting with flowers by all the back doors, little round bistro tables with two wrought-iron chairs set around the courtyard, and lush greenery looking as if someone had just draped it casually round the doorways.

'It's hard to believe we're in the middle of the city, isn't it?' she asked. 'But Eloise says we're ten minutes from the Champs-Élysées and fifteen minutes from Montmartre on the Métro.'

'It's not what I expected,' he said with a smile. When she'd told him she'd booked a budget apartment in the north of the city, he'd expected the building to be in the middle of an industrial area rather than anywhere like this hidden paradise.

There was a key safe set discreetly by the side of the door. Fizz tapped in the code, retrieved the door keys, and opened the door to let them into the atrium. The floor was polished wood planks; the walls were painted cream; and there was an old-fashioned radiator under the window, painted a dark green. The stairs were also plain wood, with a polished wooden banister and wrought-iron balustrades painted the same dark green as the radiator.

So far, so good, Oliver thought.

He followed her up the stairs, and then had to blink when she unlocked the door to reveal a tiny, tiny room. 'I thought you said you'd booked an apartment?'

'It's more like a studio,' she said. 'A bedroom, living room and kitchen in one.'

Only one bed.

He forced himself not to think about that. 'Fizz, am I being dense? Only I can't see a kitchen. There's a kettle on top of that cupboard, but a kettle doesn't really count as a kitchen.'

'Hang on.' She opened the door of the small cupboard. There was a mini fridge; the curtain on the other side of the cupboard door pulled back to reveal shelves containing a microwave, glasses and crockery. 'Ta-da! One kitchen.'

Just as well they were only in Paris for the weekend and would hardly be in the apartment long enough to drink coffee, he thought. The bed took up most of the rest of the space in the room; there were two tiny chairs and a bistro table by the window, which he assumed was meant to be the 'living room' section of the studio.

His expression must've said it all for him, because she winced. 'Sorry, Oli. I assumed there would be a bed and a sofa, and I would've taken the sofa because you're taller than me. But at least it's a *big* double bed. And I'm fairly sure I don't snore. We can cope with sharing a bed for two nights, can't we?'

'Yes.' Just as long as he didn't do anything stupid, like kiss her good morning because his brain hadn't switched on properly.

He couldn't even avoid the risk by offering to sleep on the floor, because there just wasn't enough space to do that. 'But don't complain if I snore,' he said.

'I promise. We can argue later over who sleeps on which side,' she said, and deposited her backpack on one of the chairs. He followed suit, putting his own luggage on the other chair.

'Let's go and explore,' she said.

Oliver wasn't going to let himself think about that bed. Or about what Fizz would look like, all sleepy and with her corn-coloured hair loose and spread across the pillow instead of being in a braid. 'Paris in the spring. We have flowers to find,' he said.

Oliver wasn't a snob, but he came from a wealthy background. He was used to space, Fizz reminded herself. His reaction to their weekend apartment had been a bit on the grumpy side, but she rather thought that owed more to the fact he was worried sick about his dad's health—not to mention the fact that he was supposed to be finding himself someone to settle down with.

But he seemed happy enough to walk beside her right now.

'Look—*muguet*,' she said, gesturing to the little pots of lily-of-the-valley outside the local florists. 'They're so pretty. And they smell divine. I'd love to take a pot home.'

'You'd need a lot of paperwork, first,' Oliver reminded her.

One of her friends was a florist, and Fizz remembered her talking about the certificates and licence she needed for any stock she brought in from outside England. 'Sadly, you're right.' She took a snap on her phone. 'I'll have to content myself with photos.'

They took the underground out to the Champ de Mars, and she caught her breath when she saw all the trees; the fat, fluffy clumps of bright pink flowers were the perfect counterpoint to the blue spring sky. 'I love this,' she said.

He seemed to have lost his grumpiness, now, his expression showing that he was enjoying the cherry blossom as much as she was. He took photos of her under the blossom, so she could send them to Darcy and her parents, and then the touristy shot she'd wanted of herself 'lifting' the Eiffel Tower in the palm of her hand. 'That's such a terrible cliché,' he said, his eyes crinkling at the corners. 'But I admit, it's cute.'

'Now you,' she insisted.

He groaned, but went along with it.

'I don't think we're going to climb the Tower just yet,' she said, grimacing at the long queues.

'Later is definitely a good idea,' he said. 'And maybe buying a skip-the-line ticket. Because there isn't enough time to queue to see everything in Paris in twenty-four hours. Or even forty-eight.'

'Hmm. We'll discuss that later,' she said. 'More blossom, now.'

To her delight, they found more cherry blossom in the Tuileries, and a last bit of fuchsia-coloured magnolia in the Jardin du Palais-Royal; plus they were able to take the shots she wanted of herself pretending to grasp the top of the Louvre pyramid as if she were holding a bell.

'That queue's enormous,' she said, disappointed.

'I have a suggestion,' he said. 'How about we do the spontaneous twenty-four hours thing this weekend—but we come back at the end of the summer and do Paris my way?'

'Everything planned in advance with skip-the-line tickets?' she said.

'And a boutique hotel. And tables booked at good restaurants.'

'Which will be lovely,' she said. 'And I accept, as long as we go halves. But the whole point of Laura's list was to push me out of my comfort zone. Remind me how to have fun. Even though I like fancy restaurants as much as you do, I think Laura meant this to be about finding the unexpected. Looking for joy in simple things—good bread and cheese from a market stall, eaten in a park with flowers all around. And what you were saying earlier about persuading people to let us have a sneak peek at courtyards that aren't open to the public.'

He put his arm round his shoulders and squeezed. 'You're absolutely right, and I apologise. We'll do this your way. No reservations or skip-the-line.'

'Apart from the Musée d'Orsay,' she said. 'Though I haven't forgotten that you promised to find me a violet *macaron*.'

'I will.' He laughed. 'I know better than to deprive you of cake.'

'You're just as much of a cake fiend as I am,' she reminded him.

'As long as it's more cake than frosting. I hate sickly frosting. Where next?' he asked.

'Over there.' She gestured to a wrought-iron railing which had purple wisteria cascading down it. 'This is heavenly. And very Instagrammable.'

He took more photographs, and they wandered through the streets, enjoying the blooms.

'I thought you were teasing about roses. I really didn't expect to find any here at this time of year,' she said, spotting delicate pink damask roses climbing up a railing.

'These are Pierre de Ronsard roses,' he said. 'Paris is famous for them. You'll see them in gardens, on balconies in terracotta pots, climbing up arbours.'

She walked over to them and sniffed one. 'That's the most glorious scent. Who were they named after? The horticulturalist who bred the rose?'

'No—de Ronsard was a French Renaissance poet. I did some of his poems for A level, and I still remember the first bit of his *Ode à Cassandre*.' He smiled at her. *'"Mignonne, allons voir si la rose/Qui ce matin avait déclose/Sa robe de pourpre au Soleil..."'*

She translated mentally: *Sweetheart, let's go see if the rose/Which this morning has disclosed/Her purple dress to the sun...*

It was a lovely image, but what surprised her was her reaction to Oliver's voice. Speaking in French, he sounded slightly husky and incredibly sexy.

But this was her best friend.

Sex didn't come into their relationship.

She loved him dearly, but she'd never really thought of him as a lover. Not even that one time they'd shared a kiss... And she'd better not start letting her thoughts go in that direction! Not now, when they were sharing a bed tonight in a very tiny apartment indeed...

What the hell had possessed him to quote that poem? Oliver thought. The next lines were about the rose petals falling, which the poet described as the rose losing her dress. And now he couldn't get the image out of his head: Fizz wearing a pretty sundress the same colour as the de Ronsard rose, peeling the spaghetti straps from her shoulders and the dress floating to the ground like the petals of a rose...

He went hot all over.

This was impossible. He needed to get

things back on an even keel before she guessed at what was going on in his head. 'It's actually about how beauty fades quickly. I guess it's the French equivalent to Herrick's *"Gather ye rosebuds"*.'

'Carpe diem,' she said. 'The posh guy's attempt at seduction.'

'Hey. Shakespeare did it, too, and he wasn't posh. "Come kiss me, sweet and twenty."' He stopped, aware that he was digging himself into a deeper and deeper hole, here. Fizz had been sweet and twenty when she'd kissed him and ruined him for all other women. 'The roses are pretty, anyway,' he said gruffly.

'They are,' she said.

'And what you said earlier about eating good bread and cheese in the park...' He glanced at his watch. 'Let's go and find some.' Food was safe, at least.

They found a little street market where they bought bread, cheese and a pot of olives; they were passing a fruit stall when Fizz stopped. 'I thought strawberries were *fraises*?'

'They are.'

She pointed to the sign. 'Why are they listed as *gariguettes*?'

'I'll buy some and ask,' he said.

The stallholder selected a punnet for him

and explained; Oliver headed back to Fizz. 'Apparently it's a really old variety—they're very early, and it's something to do with the elongated shape that makes them taste very sweet and juicy.'

'Perfect,' she said with a smile.

They walked back to the Tuileries, where people were gathered round the fountains in the park, sitting on the slatted green metal benches and enjoying the sun and the scent of the flowers. They managed to find a bench to enjoy their bread and cheese; and the *gariguettes* lived up to their promise, too.

After a wander through the Musée d'Orsay—where they both found favourite paintings, and Oliver snapped pictures of Fizz doing the tourist pose by the clock—they headed for the Marais.

'According to the internet, this used to be marshland,' Fizz said, checking her phone. 'Though I guess you already knew that.'

He nodded. 'A lot of the mansions were built in the seventeenth and eighteenth centuries. I think you'll love the architecture round here, and it's worth having a wander round the Place des Vosges. It's the oldest public park in Paris.' It was a place he particularly liked, and he was pretty sure Fizz would love it, too: a gorgeous square with a fountain, edged with perfectly manicured trees, in the middle of houses with slate roofs, tall windows and arched passageways. 'You'll definitely get good photos here for your parents and Darcy.'

They explored the shops and galleries, people-watched and drank coffee; and he found a shop selling *macarons* in all different colours. 'I know this is meant to be on Laura's budget, but I promised you a violet *macaron*. Wait here.'

He came back with a whole rainbow of *macarons* for her.

'Oh, now this is clever,' she said. 'I should've guessed you'd do this.'

He took a snap of her with the rainbow of *macarons* in front of her. 'One for your album,' he said.

'I'll make Darcy, Mum and Dad guess the flavours,' she said with a grin.

'Actually, that's a good idea. I challenge you to guess the flavours before you try them,' he said, and had to suppress the sudden mental image of Fizz leaning against the bench with her eyes closed while he fed her bite by bite. What was wrong with him?

'It's very obvious. Strawberry, orange, lemon,

pistachio, blueberry, blackcurrant, violet,' she said, pointing to each one in turn.

'You are so wrong,' he said. 'I should've put a forfeit in there for every one you get wrong.' *A kiss.* Oh, for pity's sake. He had to stop this. It seemed that food wasn't a safe subject, after all. In fact, no subject felt safe. He was going to have to keep a rein on his tongue.

'Forfeits are fine by me. I'll cook you dinner one evening when we're back in London for every one I get wrong,' she said. 'And you cook me dinner for every one I get right.'

'Deal.'

'And you have to share them with me,' she said, lifting up the red *macaron.* 'I'd say this is strawberry. Unless you've been very clever and bought rose instead, given that the last one is very obviously violet.'

'One *macaron,* one guess,' he said reprovingly. 'No cheating or ever so slightly bending the rules, Felicity Bennett.'

'Strawberry.' She bit into it, and he had to stop himself watching her mouth. 'It's raspberry—well, that's near enough to strawberry, isn't it?'

'No, it isn't. First point to me,' he said, accepting the half a macaron from her. 'Oh, this is good. Nice and tart. I hate the super-sweet ones.'

'Orange,' she said, taking the second. 'Oh, it's passionfruit! I love this. I think this might be the best flavour ever. And we need to have passionfruit martinis tonight. Can we find a rooftop bar, somewhere to watch the sun set?'

'Can't you have the cocktails and I can have a glass of decent red wine instead?' he asked plaintively.

'Nope. Laura's rules, I'm afraid. She even sketched a martini glass next to the task. I bet she did on Darcy's, too. Passionfruit martini was our sisterly drink. And you're with me, this weekend, so you're on the passionfruit martinis as well.'

He thought Fizz might be bluffing; but she was smiling and clearly having fun, which made him happy, so he went along with it. 'Cocktails it is,' he said.

The yellow *macaron* was pineapple rather than lemon; the green one was pistachio and orange blossom, which made her crow in triumph and amused him highly; and the blue one stumped her.

'It's a Marie Antoinette,' he said.

'And I was supposed to guess that *how*, exactly?' she asked indignantly, her hands on her hips as she gave him a mock glare. 'That's rampant cheating, Oliver Harrison, and you know it.' She took another nibble. 'I can't work out what's in the ganache. Honey, I think.'

'It's the Marie Antoinette tea, so it's meant to be tea and roses as well.' He tried it gingerly. 'Hmm. I still think the raspberry one's the best one,' he said.

'Nope. *This* one is,' she said after biting into the violet *macaron*. 'I'm afraid I don't think I can share this one with you, Oli.'

'Fair enough. Be greedy,' he teased.

She closed her eyes in bliss, clearly enjoying every morsel, and he couldn't resist snapping a picture that he most definitely wasn't going to share with her.

'That was a really lovely thing to do, Oli,' she said when she'd finished. 'Thank you for spoiling me.'

'That's what best friends are supposed to do,' he said with a smile. 'And you're the one spoiling me, whisking me off to Paris for the weekend.'

'In the smallest flat in the world, with a micro-kitchen,' she chuckled.

'And there isn't anyone else I'd rather share it with,' he said.

She beamed at him. 'Me, neither. Now, while you were buying macarons and coffee, I looked up good places to see cherry blossom. The Jardin des Plantes isn't far from here, is it?'

'No.'

'Apparently it has the biggest cherry tree in Paris.'

He stood up and held out his arm to her. 'Come with me, *mademoiselle*. Let's go and find you some more cherry blossom.'

She laughed and took his arm.

How could something be so perfect and such torture, all at the same time? He loved having her close; yet he wanted her closer still, and he couldn't find the words to tell her. It was madness to even contemplate it.

They found the enormous cherry tree Fizz had seen on the internet, and she insisted on taking selfies of them together under it. A slight breeze sent a cascade of petals over them, and for a crazy moment it felt as if someone was throwing confetti over them. He caught her eye, and it felt as if all the breath had been knocked out of his body. Had she thought it, too?

But he couldn't risk the best friendship he'd ever had. Particularly now, when she was doing the first task on Laura's bucket list and her emotions were all over the place. She needed this to be wonderful.

So he kept it light; although they didn't manage to get a ticket for a boat trip, he found a tiny restaurant with a view of the Eiffel Tower and made sure that she had the view, so she could see the Tower sparkling on the hour. The food was wonderful—a perfectly spiced veggie tagine served with flatbreads, followed by tiny sweet pastries with good coffee.

But he wasn't ready to go back to their apartment, just yet.

'I've been thinking,' he said. 'I know you wanted to do cocktails, but could this trip include dancing beside the Seine?'

'Seriously? That's a real thing, not just an urban myth?'

'It's real a thing,' he said. 'Tango and salsa.'

She looked at her canvas shoes. 'I really ought to be wearing strappy heels for dancing.'

'You can dance in anything,' he said. 'Do anything: isn't that what the Bennett sisters do?'

She met his gaze for a long, long moment, then smiled. 'Yeah. All right. Let's do the cocktails tomorrow and go dancing tonight.'

They walked along the Seine until they found the little semi-circular dance areas around the

Jardin Tino Rossi. People were dancing in the centre to sensual tango music, while others sat on the steps and watched.

'Can you tango?' he asked.

'No. Laura loved that film with Antonio Banderas dancing the tango,' she said. 'So I kind of know what it's meant to look like, but I've never done it.' She smiled. 'Darcy said she's thinking about taking ballroom dance lessons as part of her bucket list thing.'

'Is that the committing to something task?'

She shook her head. 'Apparently, it's the thing she's scared of.'

'Well, if she's got two left feet,' Oliver said, 'I kind of get it. It's daunting when everyone else can do something and you can't.'

'People are too busy having fun to notice someone getting a few steps wrong,' she said. 'If Darcy had been in London, I would've gone to the class with her, for moral support. But I'll text her.' She gestured to the dancers. 'They're amazing. I guess we could always grab a drink and just watch them.'

'Or you could follow my lead and we'll join them,' he said. 'Or let's find somewhere with something a bit less complicated like a waltz.'

'You can tango and waltz?' She looked at him in surprise. The way he'd talked earlier about dancing being daunting, it had sounded as if he had two left feet. 'Since when?' She knew everything about her best friend—or so she'd thought. She'd had no idea that he could do formal dancing.

'My first year at uni.'

Three years before she'd met him.

'There was a charity thing. A local dance school was giving lessons, and it seemed like a good idea at the time. I haven't done it for years, though, so expect me to be a bit rusty,' he warned.

The sudden shyness in his smile made her heart skip a beat. Which was absurd, because this was Oliver Harrison, her best friend. She wasn't meant to feel like that about him.

'OK. What do we do?' she asked, striving to sound normal.

'Let's find the place where they're waltzing.' In the next semicircle, she could see dancers spinning round, and it looked gorgeous; at the same time, the footwork looked a bit daunting. For the first time, she realised why her oldest sister might have been scared of dancing.

But Fizz didn't have to be scared. She had Oli.

He talked her through the dance hold and

walked her through the steps, keeping them out of the dance floor so she didn't feel pressured.

Two songs later, any suggestion of rustiness on his part was completely gone. And she trusted him not to let her mess this up. 'Let's do it,' she said.

Somehow, the tinny taped music had been replaced by someone playing an accordion and someone else playing a violin. And it felt very different, dancing under the lights and the stars on the flat paved semicircle, the river swishing gently next to them. Even though they were in the middle of a crowd, Oli was the only person she was aware of. His strength, the way he led her round the floor, the unexpected whooshy feel when he spun her round—as if he'd swept her off her feet, yet at the same time he managed to keep her safely grounded. His gracefulness as they moved around the floor, his steps effortless and sure.

It made her breathless, something she wasn't used to where Oli was concerned. Sensual. Close. Her pulse throbbed with the violin, staccato and much quicker than usual, but it wasn't the physical effort of dancing. With shock, she realised it was the dance itself. With Oliver. Cheek to cheek, their bodies pressed close, the rise and fall of the dance.

If he could have this effect on her when they were both dressed casually, what would it be like to dance with him in proper ballroom clothing? A dark suit and a crisp white shirt, with herself in heels and a red silk dress that billowed out when he spun her round...

And he was so close. She could feel the warmth of his body against hers, feel the drumming of his own heartbeat. And his cheek was against hers. If both of them moved just the tiniest fraction, their lips would be touching.

Her mouth tingled.

A kiss...

She was only aware that the song had ended because of the applause from the other dancers.

Dear God. She'd never forgotten herself like that before when she'd been out dancing. Never been swept away in the moment. Never felt suddenly head over heels.

Maybe it was starting the bucket list that had stirred up her emotions, but she was seeing Oliver with very different eyes right now—and it was scary. Way out of her comfort zone. He wasn't just the geek with a passion for art who could make you see all the things you'd never noticed before in a painting, or the man with an eye for detail who seemed to just snap his fingers and turn a logistical mess into something smoothly organised with the minimum of effort. Right now, he was all male. The thing she'd never really let herself see before.

And she had no idea where this was going to lead.

CHAPTER THREE

IT HAD BEEN a while since Oliver had danced like this, and it made him feel giddy to be this close to Fizz. He'd forgotten just how sexy a waltz could feel. And then there was the rest of it: the last remnants of the sunset fading into the night, the lights sparkling and reflecting on the water as it darkened to reflect the sky, the romance of the music...and her nearness. It would be oh, so easy to kiss her right now; but they were sharing a room tonight. *Sharing a bed.* It wouldn't be fair to put that kind of pressure on her.

So he kept himself under strict control.

They'd been dancing for nearly an hour when he noticed that she was starting to droop.

'Come on, Sleeping Beauty. I'll call us a cab,' he said.

She shook her head. 'I'll be fine on the underground.'

He stroked her cheek. 'You were up ridiculously early this morning. I know you want to do everything on your budget, and I respect that, but will you let me take you back to the apartment by taxi? Because I worry about you, Fizz. You can't burn the candle at both ends and be OK. And I'm sure Laura would bend her rules so you get to see the city all lit up.'

He could see the indecision on her face, but eventually she nodded. 'All right. Thank you.'

When their cab arrived, he asked the driver to take them through the city rather than on the ring road, even though it would take a few minutes longer, because he wanted to give Fizz the chance to see some of the famous buildings lit up at night. They drove along the quayside, where the lights were reflected on the Seine; across the Pont de la Concorde, where the obelisk was lit up in front of them; past the Louvre and the Palais Garnier, the buildings looking stunning in the spotlights; and past Sacré-Coeur shining like a white beacon on its hill.

'I can see why they call Paris the City of Light,' Fizz said. 'It's so beautiful at night.'

Oliver took her hand. 'This is a bit slower than the underground, but I thought you'd enjoy this. It's kind of making up for not being able to get tickets for a river trip.'

'And how,' she said. 'You've made Paris special for me, Oli.'

'Good.'

Back at their flat, he said, 'You have the bathroom first. Do you want me to make you a hot drink—a chamomile tea or something?'

'No. I'm all right,' she said. 'But thank you for the offer. And I'm sorry I'm cramping your style a bit. You could probably have danced until midnight and not even noticed the time.'

'It's fine. You can remind me of that tomorrow morning when you have to wake me up and I'm grumpy,' he said with a smile. 'Or when you tell me I kept you awake all night.' Oh, hell. The pictures *that* put in his head. 'By snoring,' he added hastily.

She emerged from the bathroom wearing shorts and a strappy vest as her pyjamas. Oliver was extremely grateful for the fact the hot water ran out halfway through his own shower, because the coldness of the water shocked some common sense back into his head. And he was even more grateful to discover that Fizz had already fallen asleep by the time he walked back into their room.

He turned the light out, climbed into bed as gently as he could so he wouldn't wake her, and lay there with his eyes wide open, wishing he could fall asleep as easily as she had. And it was fine until she turned over in her sleep and then shifted so her back was against him. How could he resist turning onto his side and spooning against her, sliding an arm round her waist? He breathed in the scent of her hair and remembered how it felt to dance with her, how much the sensuality of the movement had got to him and made him want to kiss her.

He was in big trouble. He'd buried his feelings for Fizz for so long; why were they surfacing now? Maybe here in Paris he'd find the words to tell her how he felt—and in a way that didn't mean he'd lose his best friend.

The next morning, Fizz woke to find herself wrapped in Oliver's arms, her legs tangled with his. Yesterday morning, she'd thought it a bit of a joke that they were going to share a bed, but today it felt like something different. Particularly after the way he'd tangoed with her on the banks of the river. She'd been so close to kissing him.

Except he didn't feel that way about her, did he? They'd always been the best of friends. Apart from that one night when she'd told him about Laura's prognosis and they'd ended up kissing; but he'd been the one to pull back, telling her that she was vulnerable right then and he wouldn't take advantage of her because he respected her too much. She'd thought at the time that maybe he was trying to reject her as kindly as he could and keep her firmly in the friend zone.

Besides, if he really was attracted to her, surely he would've remembered that kiss—and last night, when they'd danced, his control would've been as shaky as hers. But he hadn't kissed her last night either, had he?

Maybe she was just overthinking things.

This was meant to be a few hours out of normal time, where they had fun in a city he knew relatively well but she'd never visited. A wild twenty-four hours, not a wild fling. They were doing this as friends.

But, right at this moment, Oliver Harrison didn't feel like her best friend.

It felt as if they were on the verge of being something else entirely. And she wasn't sure if that scared her or thrilled her.

He was still asleep; she watched him for a little while. How long his lashes were, and how beautiful he was in repose; it made her itch to sketch him. Sculpt him, even.

She shook herself. This was dangerous. She didn't want to wreck the closest relationship she had outside her parents and her sister. Right now, it would be sensible to put some distance between them and get her head straight, so she could face him again on their usual best-friend terms. Very gently, without waking him, she wriggled out of his arms and slipped on her clothes.

The last time she'd woken in bed with someone, he'd been a stranger rather than someone who knew her almost better than she knew herself. Shame and guilt had piled on top of her grief, that morning. The whole thing had been a mess, tangled up with the worst moments of her life. She'd never spoken about it to anyone, and she wasn't going to start now. She shoved the memories aside, scribbled a note for Oliver saying that she'd gone to pick up breakfast, and headed out in search of buttery croissants.

The *boulangerie* that the owner of the apartment had recommended sold a variety of pastries as well as croissants and bread, plus *macarons* made with bitter chocolate that she knew were Oliver's favourite. She bought a small box of *macarons* to give him once they were back in London and a selection of pastries, then headed to a nearby café to have her water bottle filled with freshly squeezed orange juice and the two reusable cups with good coffee.

Oliver was still asleep when she got back. She set everything on the small bistro table, then tapped him gently on the shoulder. 'Hey, Sleeping Beauty. Time for breakfast.'

'Uh…' He squeezed his eyes shut, then sighed. 'OK. Thank you. I don't expect you to wait on me hand and foot.'

'I know. See you at the table when you're ready.'

He dragged himself out to the table; they'd breakfasted together in pyjamas a few times, when one of them had stayed in the other's spare room, but today felt different. Which was utterly ridiculous. She gulped orange juice to hide her confusion.

'The pastries look nice,' he said. He took a sip of the coffee. 'Oh, that's *good*.'

It didn't take long for the coffee to kick in. Oliver insisted on doing the washing up before he had a quick shower and dressed in the bathroom; meanwhile, Fizz sent a selection of the photographs she'd taken yesterday to Darcy and her parents.

Enjoying Laura's bucket list in Paris. Raising a cocktail to her tonight. Have stuffed face with a rainbow of macarons, seen some of the sights, seen the Eiffel Tower sparkling at night and tan-goed next to the Seine.

Darcy replied almost immediately.

You took Oliver to Paris?

Well, it was a bit late for her to be upset about it now. If they'd opened their lists together, maybe they could've done some of it together. She pushed down the flash of irritation. Darcy was as messed up as she was.

She texted back, trying to be conciliatory.

Sorry. If you want to do Paris with me, we can go when you're free.

Might be going to Rome for Laura's list.

Darcy wasn't asking Fizz to go with her?

She damped down the twinge of hurt, typing back.

That's a bit cryptic. Going with...?

The ensuing radio silence made her narrow her eyes. If Darcy wanted to be cagey, there wasn't a lot she could do about it. 'Laura, I wish you were here. I think we need you to glue us back together. We can't do it ourselves,' she said with a sigh.

'Can't do what yourselves?' Oliver asked, walking back into the main room and clearly overhearing the last sentence.

In response, Fizz handed him her phone.

'Fizz, you can't really tell someone's tone from a text message,' Oliver said gently. 'She's not necessarily upset that you asked me to go with you instead of her. And she's not knocking you back. Maybe she's met someone and she's not ready to talk about it yet, in case she jinxes it. I've never met anyone else who was jilted at the altar, but it must really make it hard to trust anyone again once it's happened to you.'

'She barely dates,' Fizz agreed.

'The two of you need to sit down and talk,' Oliver said. 'But not now. Right this minute, you're in Paris, on Laura's orders—and I believe the flea market awaits.'

'Proper bargain hunting,' she said. 'You might even find an undiscovered Modigliani.'

He laughed. 'I doubt that, not even a sketch— but you might find some interesting jewellery you can take apart and reset.'

They left the apartment to discover that the

famous flea market really was right on their doorstep. The stalls displayed their wares to the browsers, everything from stands of copper pans to stalls of little tables. There were gilt chairs with striped pastel chintz upholstery, shelves of gleaming silverware and glass, and walls filled with mirrors and paintings and framed sketches—though not one of the originals she'd teased Oliver about—and stacks of empty frames. Old-fashioned suitcases opened to reveal vintage toys and battered teddy bears; other stalls had baskets to rummage through.

Fizz couldn't resist buying an old-fashioned manual coffee grinder shaped like a box with a handle on the top and drawer to collect the grounds. Then her alarm rang on her phone.

'Two hours. That's enough flea market shopping,' she said.

'What do you want to do now?' Oliver asked.

'Let's drop this back at the apartment, so we don't have to carry it all round the city,' she said, gesturing to her coffee grinder. 'And then I think we'll look for street art.'

'La Butte aux Cailles is meant to be amazing,' he said.

'Then that's where we'll go.'

There turned out to be lots of street art, from a prowling tiger with turquoise eyes to a child skipping and looking as if her knees had vanished through the wall, seeming almost three-dimensional with the 'shadow' of the skipping rope. Fizz was drawn by a wall of sunflowers, and Oliver spotted a balloon. 'Which is fitting,' he said, 'because this was where the Montgolfier brothers' first hot air balloon landed.'

'It doesn't feel anything like the wide boulevards in the middle of Paris,' Fizz said. 'It's more like a village.' The streets were narrower and cobbled, the small front gardens of the terraced houses filled with greenery or bursting with spring flowers.

'It's more like parts of Notting Hill than Paris,' Oliver agreed.

Further on, it felt even more like a village, with beautiful old-fashioned streetlamps and pastel wooden shutters against the cream-painted walls.

'The Canal Saint-Martin's meant to be lovely, too,' she said. 'We can stop for lunch at a café, walk a bit under the chestnut trees, and then head for Montmartre.'

'Fine by me,' he said.

They found a patisserie with wide canvas

awnings and fancy lettering; the queue for the takeaway section told them just how good the food was. Fortified by a traditional croque monsieur served with a rocket and baby plum tomato salad, they wandered along the banks of the Canal Saint-Martin, her arm tucked through his. She was glad the scratchy awkwardness of this morning had gone, and she had her best friend back, to tease and laugh with.

'Alfred Sisley painted along here,' Oliver said. 'The invisible Impressionist.'

'Didn't we see some of his paintings yesterday at the Musée d'Orsay?' Fizz asked.

'Yes. What I mean is he's a bit overshadowed by Monet and Renoir—they were friends of his, and he was one of the founding members of the Impressionists, but they had a lot more success. The last few years of his life were pretty rough.'

'Pretty standard for painters in Paris,' she said. 'Think about Van Gogh, Picasso, Modigliani.'

'Some of Sisley's paintings were gorgeous, though,' Oliver said. 'There's one in the National, a view of the Thames at Charing Cross Bridge—I love the sky in that one.'

'Maybe we can go and see it when we're back in London,' she said.

'I'd like that,' he said.

They caught the Métro to Montmartre and climbed the steps all the way up to the Sacré-Coeur. They wandered towards the Place du Tertre; the pretty square at the top of the hill was stuffed with stalls showcasing the work of artists, everything from postcard-sized pencil sketches through to oil landscapes.

'Apparently there's a ten-year waiting list to get a pitch here, and the pitches are shared by artists on alternate days,' Oliver said.

There were buskers, too—a violinist playing Fauré, a man with an accordion playing Aznavour, and a guitarist playing Satie.

'I love it,' Fizz said. 'I can imagine living and working here.'

'It's even lovely in the rain,' Oliver said. 'Come and see Utrillo's pink house.'

On the corner of two cobbled streets, La Maison Rose lived up to its name: bright pink, with green shutters and doors.

'That's charming,' Fizz said. 'And, oh, the wisteria! That's glorious.'

Oliver took some snaps of her along the cobbled street with the wisteria in the background.

'I think this is my favourite bit of Paris,' she said. 'And I'm guessing it's yours, too.'

'Pretty much on a par with the Marais. That timer you had on your phone—you'd *definitely* need that if you let me browse those stalls back in the Place du Tertre,' he said.

She grinned. 'More likely, we'd laugh and ignore it because I'd be right there with you.'

'We need coffee,' he said. 'And a pastry. And a sketch.'

'In that order,' Fizz said.

There was a nearby patisserie with an enormous display in a glass cabinet; Fizz found it hard to choose, but eventually picked a Paris Brest: choux pastry shaped like a bicycle wheel and filled with piped praline cream, topped with flaked almonds and icing sugar. 'This is wonderful,' she said after her first mouthful. 'Want to try some?'

'No, and you can keep your beady eyes off my *tarte au citron*,' Oliver retorted with a teasing grin.

'Spoilsport,' she pouted.

He loaded up a forkful. 'Actually, this is probably the best lemon tart I've ever tasted. So I'll be nice. You can try it.'

And there it was again as he held the forkful of lemon tart out to her: that little flash of sensualism. As if he were a lover, feeding her treats...

She really needed to get a grip. Especially as she could feel the betraying colour flushing through her cheeks. Would he notice? Did she *want* him to notice?

'Fabulous,' she said, and hoped that he'd put her blush down to a sugar rush or something similar. The last thing she wanted to do right now was admit to this weird feeling; though, at the same time, it intrigued her. It was something she didn't think she'd ever feel.

They found an artist to sketch them together in charcoal, and sat smiling at each other as the artist worked; he rolled the drawing and slotted it into a cardboard tube to keep it safe from damage. And then they wandered through Montmartre, exploring the gorgeous cobbled streets and stopping to take photographs of places where the famous painters had lived and worked, loved and laughed and despaired, a hundred or so years before.

After dinner of chicken chasseur with bulgar wheat and buttery, garlicky spinach in a traditional little bistro with red and white checked tablecloths, bentwood chairs and raffia-covered bottles used as candleholders, they found a rooftop bar with an amazing view over the city. On one side was the Sacré-Coeur; on the other, they could see the Eiffel Tower.

'This is just *perfect*,' Fizz said, settling into one of the wicker chairs.

'I believe *mademoiselle* was insisting that we should both have passionfruit martinis tonight?' Oliver asked.

'We're in Paris, so I suppose we really ought to drink something that's properly Parisian, instead,' she said.

'Pernod or pastis? Or maybe absinthe,' he suggested.

'Isn't absinthe banned?' she asked.

'No, that's a myth. And it's not hallucinogenic, either,' he said. 'It's just a really high proof, so people get drunk more quickly on it.'

She couldn't help smiling. 'Oli, you're such a geek. How do you know all this stuff?'

'In-flight magazines can be surprisingly interesting,' he said. 'Hemingway apparently invented a cocktail in Paris named after his book, *Death in the Afternoon*—absinthe and champagne.'

'What's actually in absinthe?' she asked.

'Hang on, and I'll tell you.' He looked it up. 'Wormwood, fennel and star anise. I've never actually drunk it, but apparently it's quite bitter, which is why it's served with a sugar lump.'

'Well, this is meant to be a wild time in Paris—let's try absinthe,' she said. 'Both of us.'

Oliver had a word with the barman, who brought over a tray and set up the drink for them. There was a clear green liquid in the bottom of the two glasses; he balanced a flat spoon with a slatted bowl on the glasses, and a sugar lump on top of that.

'This is the absinthe fountain,' the barman said, putting a contraption between their glasses that looked a bit like an old-fashioned lantern glass, filled with ice cubes and water. There were four tiny taps running from it. 'You drip the water really slowly onto the sugar cube until it dissolves,' he explained. 'It goes cloudy, like Pastis or Pernod. And then, when the sugar is dissolved, it will be ready to drink.'

'*Merci beaucoup,*' Oliver said.

'So this is *la fée verte,*' Fizz said. 'OK.'

Oliver took photographs of her with the absinthe fountain working, and then took a photograph of her as she was about to taste the drink.

She almost choked on her first mouthful.

'How could the artists possibly have drunk this stuff?' she asked, grimacing.

'It's that bad?' Oliver asked.

'Uh. Try it and tell me.'

He did so. 'That's possibly not my favourite,' he said.

'It's absolutely revolting, Oli. Admit it,' she demanded.

'An acquired taste, maybe.' He returned her grimace. 'I'll ask the barman if there's a sweeter Parisian cocktail you might like—if not, do you want your usual?'

She smiled. 'Yes, please.'

He sent the photographs over to her and took the drinks and the fountain back to the barman. Fizz forwarded the pictures to her parents and Darcy.

Absinthe sounds much, much nicer than it tastes! More like la fée bleugh than la fée verte! xx

Oliver came back a few moments later with two martini glasses. One held an amber liquid, garnished with strips of orange peel, and the other was pink with a foamy top, garnished with a raspberry.

'A 1789,' he said, nodding at the amber one, 'and a French martini. I'm assuming you'll try both, so start with the 1789 because it's the less sweet one.'

Even a small sip made her catch her breath. 'What's in it?'

'French whisky, white wine and a French citrus aperitif,' he said.

'It's a lot better than the absinthe, but still not *quite* my thing,' she said.

'That's why I suggested you try that one first.' He smiled. 'You'll love the other one.'

'I'm sure my gran used to drink something she said was a French martini,' Fizz said pensively, 'and it was vile. Though it wasn't frothy.'

'I know the stuff you mean,' he said. 'I had an aunt who loved it, too. She used to mix it with lemonade.'

'So did my gran.' Gingerly, she tasted the cocktail. 'Oh, my God. That's definitely *not* what she used to drink. This is fantastic! It's even better than a passionfruit martini. I need to know what's in this so I can make one for Darcy.'

'Vodka, pineapple juice and black raspberry liqueur, shaken over big lumps of ice—that's what gives the frothy bit at the top,' he said. 'Give me your phone. I need to take a picture of you smiling like that, before your sister hunts me down and kills me for letting you drink absinthe. Because I'm assuming you told her how bad it tastes.'

She laughed, and he took the snap.

'"French martini,"' she read aloud as she typed in the caption. '"Better even than passionfruit. Oli's suggestion."' She pressed 'send'. 'You're safe from her wrath, now,' she said with a smile.

'Good. Darcy's scary.'

'She's a pussycat,' Fizz protested.

'Not where her baby sister's happiness is concerned,' Oliver said. 'I know you worry that you've drifted apart, but deep down I don't think you have.'

She trusted his judgement—Oliver had always been astute—and it took a lot of the sting out of how she'd felt after seeing the solicitor with Darcy on Laura's anniversary.

He stuck to wine, after that, and she tried several more different cocktails. And she was glad she was wearing canvas shoes rather than heels when she almost tripped on the way back to the Métro.

Oliver put his arm round her. 'Let's make sure you stay upright.'

'Sure,' she said, and grinned at him. It didn't feel like it usually did when Oliver gave her a hug, but it was a new kind of nice. She found herself sliding her arm round his waist in return; and, even on the Métro, he didn't let go of her. She couldn't remember the last time she'd felt this cherished, and it warmed her all the way through. It made her want to dance through the streets.

'I do love you, you know, Oli,' she said, when they got back to the apartment.

'Love you, too, Fizzikins. Though in the morning I'm pretty sure you won't remember telling me this, so I promise you now that I'm not going to embarrass you by bringing it up.'

'I think the cocktails might have gone a bit to my head,' she said. That, or maybe Oliver had. Not that she was going to tell him.

'Just a little bit.' He dropped a kiss on her forehead. 'You have the bathroom first. And then I'll get you a big glass of water and you can drink it all tonight before you go to sleep, to stop you having a monstrous hangover tomorrow morning.'

'I love you,' she said again. 'And I love Paris. And I really, *really* love French martinis.'

'I know.' He laughed. 'Go get your PJs on.'

Just as he'd promised, Oliver brought Fizz a big glass of water. And, just as he'd suggested, she drank the lot. But, unlike the previous night, she was still awake when he came to bed—even though she closed her eyes and pretended to be asleep.

Since they'd been in Paris, she'd started to feel differently towards her best friend. She'd seen him in a different light: dancing sensuously with her by the river, feeding her tastes of things, and walking through the most romantic city in the world with their arms round each other.

And now he was lying next to her. In a big bed, admittedly—but it wasn't that big. They'd woken in each other's arms, this morning. What if...?

But the water had started to sober her up. He'd just told her he loved her, but she was pretty sure he meant it platonically. She didn't want to risk wrecking their friendship by making a move on him, particularly if he turned her down. And he would turn her down, she knew; he'd never take advantage of a woman who was even slightly tipsy.

All the same, she couldn't help wondering. What if she and Oliver...?

Oliver woke ridiculously early, the next morning. Fizz was snoring gently, so he knew it was safe to open his eyes; he wouldn't have to talk to her until he was properly awake and could marshal his words into a coherent order.

Last night, she'd told him that she loved him.

This morning, would she remember that? Would she remember him telling her that he loved her, too?

Though he rather thought they had different definitions of love. Fizz had always made it clear that he was her best friend and—apart from that one kiss, when he'd turned her down because she was vulnerable and he absolutely wasn't going to take advantage of her—she'd always treated him like a brother.

Maybe he was being a coward, not raising the issue. But the way he saw it, he had too much to lose. If they had *that* conversation and she turned him down, things would be awkward between them. She'd start to avoid him, and the distance between them would grow until they were nothing more than acquaintances. His life would be much flatter and duller without her. If the choice was between having her as his best friend and nothing, it was a no-brainer. He'd keep his mouth shut—and keep her in his life.

He glanced at his watch. It was still early, but it was late for Fizz to be asleep. Which probably meant that, despite the water he'd persuaded her to drink last night, she'd have a bit of a hangover. He climbed out of bed without disturbing her, dressed, left her a note to say he was fetching breakfast and crept out of the flat.

As soon as he left the courtyard, he could smell coffee and fresh-baked bread. He followed his nose and bought a baguette, on the grounds that Fizz could do with something more substantial than a croissant to mop up last night's cocktails, along with jam from a market stall, some handmade chocolates that his parents would enjoy, two takeout coffees and some paracetamol.

Fizz was awake when he got back and had clearly showered and dressed; her bag was packed, and she was sitting on the bed, using her knees as a desk for a small sketchpad.

'Working?' he asked.

'Only a teensy-tiny bit,' she said. 'I wanted to make some notes about the wisteria earrings. And I think cherry blossom earrings in pink enamel, maybe with a matching ring.'

He smiled. 'I expected you to have a hang-over.'

'From mixing those cocktails, last night? I probably deserve one,' she said, 'but, actually, I feel wonderful.'

'If that changes, I bought paracetamol,' he said. 'Plus coffee, a baguette and jam.'

'Perfect,' she said with a smile.

After they'd had breakfast at the little table overlooking the courtyard, he showered, changed and packed. They tidied the tiny apartment, put the key back in its safe box by the back door, and headed for the centre of Paris for a last look at the cherry blossom and an ice cream, before catching the train back to London.

Back at St Pancras, Fizz said, 'Thank you for coming with me to Paris, Oli. For helping me start Laura's bucket list.'

'I'm glad you asked me,' he said. 'And if I can do anything to help with the other three tasks, just tell me.'

She nodded. 'I'll call you later in the week.' And then, to his surprise, she handed him a box. 'They're the bitter chocolate ones because weirdly, for a cake fiend, you hate sweet things.'

'You really didn't need to do that, especially

as you treated me to Paris and only let me buy you a couple of drinks and some *macarons*, but thank you.' He kissed her cheek. 'Check your diary for September and let me know when you're free, because we're going back to Paris and next time we're doing it my way, all planned. My treat. No arguments.'

'All right. Thank you.' She smiled at him. 'Catch you later.'

At ten o'clock on Monday morning, Fizz was interrupted by the doorbell. A delivery driver handed her a glorious arrangement of sunflowers. She recognised the writing on the envelope, and the card that came with it confirmed it.

Thank you for Paris. Love, Oli x

She knew why he'd sent her sunflowers, too. They were Laura's favourite flower, the ones that always made Fizz smile with their brightness. The flowers that made up her signature jewellery collection.

He'd be busy at work now, so she'd call him later. In the meantime, she texted him.

Flowers gorgeous. Thank you. F xx

His reply came when he was clearly taking a break.

Least I can do. Speak soon, O xx

And it left her smiling for the rest of the day.

CHAPTER FOUR

ON TUESDAY, Fizz sat at her jeweller's bench, putting the final polish on the engagement ring she'd been working on: a central round diamond, with smaller diamonds set round it, and then a row of spaced diamonds in three-pronged claws. The overall effect was of an Art Deco sunflower. Pleased with it, she slipped it onto her left hand to see how it would look being worn; luckily, her finger was the same size as the bride's. It felt comfortable against the skin and moved easily. She turned her hand so the diamonds caught the light, and was in the middle of examining the ring critically under her loupe for anything that needed a final tweak when her phone shrilled.

She frowned as she saw Oliver's name on the screen. At this time he'd be busy at work—even more than usual, right now, as he was gearing up to take over from his father. If he was ringing her, something must be up. 'Oli? Is everything all right?' she asked.

'No,' he said. 'Mum rang me. Dad's been rushed into hospital.' He swallowed hard. 'I've called a taxi and I'm leaving the gallery now. I just wanted to let you...' His voice tailed off.

She knew that feeling. She'd been there. He was panicking that his dad might not make it, and he needed her support. Which of course she'd give him. Even if she'd been in the middle of a meeting with a client when he'd called, she would've apologised to the client and rearranged the meeting so she could be at the hospital with him. 'I'll meet you at the hospital, Oli. Which one?'

'Hampstead. The Emergency Department.'

'Got it. I'm leaving now,' she said. 'Ring me if you need me. I'll text you as soon as I know my ETA.'

She grabbed her bag, locked the front door and headed straight for the Tube station.

She was held up on the street by a mass of pedestrians moving at the slowest pace in the world. The train was just disappearing into the tunnel when she arrived on the platform, so she had to wait another three minutes; she texted Oliver to let him know that she would be there in less than twenty minutes. She checked her watch every few seconds; time seemed to be moving like treacle. But at last the train arrived and whizzed her through to Belsize Park. She'd already tapped in the hospital's address on her phone while she was waiting on the platform, so the directions were ready and she power-walked to the hospital.

Oliver hadn't texted her back, so Fizz assumed that he'd switched his phone to silent—at least, she hoped it was that and not because Mark had taken a sudden turn for the worse.

'How can I help?' the receptionist asked when Fizz got to the Emergency Department.

'I'd like to see Mark Harrison, please. He was brought here by ambulance—I think it was about an hour ago?'

'Are you family?'

Not strictly, but Fizz didn't want to risk being told to wait somewhere; Oliver needed her support. 'His son's my other half,' she fibbed. And then, wanting to back up the fib with some truth, because she didn't like lying, she added, 'He called me at work to let me know his dad's been brought in, and I said I'd meet him here.'

'All right, love. I'll just check where he is.'

The receptionist checked her computer system. 'He's been moved to the cardiac care unit.' She gave Fizz the directions.

'Thank you,' Fizz said gratefully, and went to find the Harrisons.

The receptionist at the cardiac care unit directed her to the waiting room, where Oliver was pacing up and down, and his mother, Juliet, was sitting staring numbly at a paper cup of something brown with a bit of scum on the top that was probably meant to be coffee.

'Fizz.' He wrapped his arms round her. 'Thank you for coming. I appreciate...' His voice caught, but she knew what he was trying to tell her.

'I know.' She hugged him back. When he released her, she went over to his mother and hugged her, too. 'Hi, Juliet. How are you doing? And how's Mark?'

'They're doing tests.' Juliet's breathing was shallow, and Fizz could see that the older woman was only just managing to contain her emotions. 'That's why they sent us out to wait here. But he's talking and he's making sense. Downstairs, they said they didn't think he'd had a stroke.'

'What happened?' Fizz asked.

Juliet bit her lip. 'One minute he was talking to me, and then next minute he said he felt a bit weird—and then he passed out. He'd come round again by the time the ambulance arrived, and they brought him straight here.'

'That must've been so scary for you.' Fizz sat down beside her and took one hand. 'What have they said so far?'

'Just that they think it's his heart. They can't tell us anything more until they've run the tests,' Oliver said.

'Can I go to the kiosk downstairs and get you both a decent cup of coffee?' Fizz asked.

Juliet shook her head. 'Thanks, love, but I don't really want any. I don't even know why I accepted this one.' She put the paper cup down on the table in the waiting room.

'Have you had anything to eat?' Fizz asked.

'I'm not hungry,' Juliet said.

'Same here,' Oliver agreed.

'But I *could* do with the loo,' Juliet said. 'I haven't dared leave, just in case. Will you come and get me, Fizz, if the nurse says we can go back in to see him?'

'Of course I will,' Fizz promised.

When Juliet had left the room, Fizz looked at Oliver. 'OK. What didn't you want to say in front of your mum?'

His eyes widened. 'How did you know that?'

'Because I know *you*,' she said quietly. 'Though she's in too much of a flap to have picked it up. You've got away with it.'

A muscle flickered in his jaw, betraying his tension. 'I'm scared that Dad won't get through this.'

'He's in the right place,' she said gently. 'This is a specialist ward. They're the best ones to fix whatever the problem is.'

'I know. But I can't stop thinking the worst. Even when he was first diagnosed with the cardiac arrhythmia, he was still Dad. Still strong and in control. I've never known him be anything else. I don't think I've ever even seen him cry, not even when we lost Wilf the Westie ten years ago. And now...' He closed his eyes briefly. 'Sorry. After everything you went through with Laura, I'm being self-indulgent.'

'No, you're not. He's your dad, and he collapsed. Of course you're worried,' Fizz said.

'Sorry for dragging you away from work.'

She smiled. 'Oliver Harrison, you could ring me at stupid o'clock in the morning and I wouldn't have a hissy fit on you. You're important to me. Of course I'll be there when you need me—just as you supported me when Laura was ill, and you've been there for me for the bucket list stuff. I would've been a lot more upset with you if you hadn't called me.'

'Thank you.' He gave her a wry smile. 'Sorry, I'm all over the place.'

'Which is perfectly natural. I'd be the same, in your shoes,' she said, giving him another hug. 'When did you last eat?'

'Breakfast.' He blew out a breath. 'I can't face anything now.'

She glanced at her watch. 'It might make you feel better. And you need to look after yourself if you want to be able to look after your dad.'

Just as Juliet joined them again, one of the nursing team came in. 'We've finished doing our tests on your husband, now, so you can go back to see him whenever you like. We're going to keep him in overnight and do an ablation tomorrow—that's where we use radio waves to block off the electrical circuits in his heart that aren't working properly, and that should restore his heart to a normal rhythm. No driving for at least two days, and no lifting for at least two weeks, but he should be able to go home the day after tomorrow.'

Juliet's eyes filled with tears. 'So he's going to be all right?'

'We'll do our best to make sure of it,' the

nurse said with a smile. 'It'll take him a little while to recover, but we can support him through that, too. Would you like to come and see him?'

'Definitely,' Juliet said. 'You come, too, Fizz. It'll do him good to see you.'

Mark was leaning back against the pillows, wearing a hospital gown and looking tired and drawn, but he smiled when he saw them. 'Sorry to have worried you all. Fizz, how lovely to see you. Come and sit down.'

She did so, and he took her hand. 'Did you enjoy Paris? Oliver said you'd never been before. I thought he was teasing me—how could an art student never have visited the Louvre?—but...' Then he did a double-take and stared at her left hand. 'Oh, my God. Is that an *engagement* ring?'

Oh, no. Since Oliver's call, it had completely slipped her mind that she'd been checking the ring. Before she could explain that it was a commission and she was working on it for someone else, Juliet had taken her hand and inspected the ring, too. 'Oh, that's gorgeous—it looks like a sunflower. Is it one of your own designs?' At Fizz's shocked nod, Juliet added, 'Oh, so now we know why you two *really* sneaked off to Paris for the weekend. Oliver told us a story about it being part of a bucket list thing—when you actually went there to get engaged.' She looked delighted.

'Well, that's the best news ever,' Mark said, smiling broadly. 'And if that isn't an incentive to get well soon, I don't know what is! Our boy getting married—and, best of all, getting married to someone we already love.'

Fizz looked at Oliver; his mouth was hanging open slightly.

'Over the years, we always hoped this was on the cards,' Juliet said. 'You've been such good friends for such a long time—and you fit right in with our family, Fizz.'

Oh, help.

'We really ought to have champagne to toast your news,' Mark said, 'though I'm not allowed alcohol at the moment.'

Oliver cleared his throat, seemingly coming out of his shock. 'Fizz and I will go and get some sparkling water, as the next best thing,' Oliver said, tipping his head towards the door of his dad's room and widening his eyes at Fizz.

'Good idea,' Fizz said, filled with panic and realising that Oliver was trying to get her out of the situation before his parents got completely carried away. 'We'll be back in a minute.'

'No rush,' Mark said. 'We might be ancient, but we remember what it was like to be young and in love—don't we, Jools?'

'We certainly do. Take your time,' Juliet said. Her blue eyes, so like Oliver's, were filled with joy.

As soon as they were outside the doors of the cardiac care unit, and were unlikely to be overheard by Juliet or Mark, Fizz burst out, 'Oli, I'm *so* sorry. I was working on the ring and I'd just put it on my finger for a last inspection to see if I was happy with it or if anything needed tweaking. Then you called, and I—well, I dropped everything so I could come straight out to you. I didn't even *think* about the ring.' She bit her lip. 'I'm so, so sorry. It's all my fault, so I'll explain the mistake to your parents when we get back.'

'Mum and Dad were so thrilled,' Oliver said. 'But they're going to be really upset when we tell them the truth.' He looked awkward, his mind clearly working something through. 'Fizz, I know this is a big ask, but do you think we could hold off telling them until after Dad's operation? Maybe even until he's recovered?'

She felt her eyes widen. 'You mean, pretend we really *are* engaged?'

'I know it's lying, and neither of us is in the habit of doing that; but my parents are at a really low ebb right now. Mum's only just holding it together. And you heard what Dad said about it being an incentive to him getting well. The engagement will give them both something else to focus on and help stop them worrying so much about Dad's heart.'

'The longer we leave it before we tell them, the harder it'll be to admit the truth—and the more hurt your parents will be that we lied to them,' Fizz warned.

'I know.' Oliver raked a hand through his hair, looking vulnerable. 'But they'll be in a better place to deal with it then than they are right now. It's his *heart*, Fizz. I'd never say this in front of Mum, but if he doesn't pull through the operation tomorrow…what then? Who knows how long he didn't tell us about the symptoms before he first went to see the doctor, and if being untreated for so long has weakened his heart? If we tell him the truth before the operation and the shock kills him, I'll never forgive myself. If we wait until after the operation, then if he doesn't…' He swallowed hard, and whispered, 'If he doesn't make it, at least he'll die happy.'

Even though Fizz thought this might be the worst idea in the world—and it was all her own fault—she could understand Oliver's point of view. In his shoes, wouldn't she feel the same?

'All right,' she said. 'Until he's recovered, as far as your parents are concerned, we're engaged. But then we need to tell them the truth. And I have a bride-to-be who needs this ring on Friday afternoon. That's not negotiable.'

'Could you make another one? I'll buy the materials,' he said.

To do this properly, she'd need to spend a while in Hatton Garden, matching gems and negotiating. And that would take up way too much time. 'It'd probably be quickest if I made it in silver and zircona—and I have both of those back at the flat. I can make the ring and collets fairly quickly.'

'Collets?' Oliver asked, looking confused.

'The bits of the setting that hold the jewels in place,' she said. 'Though actually it's the filing and sanding that takes the time, rather than making the initial shapes.'

'But you could do it before you have to give the ring back to its real owner?'

Given the circumstances, she'd move everything else on her list to make sure she could do it. 'Sure.'

'Thanks, Fizz.' He hugged her. 'I couldn't ask for a better fake fiancée.'

'Same here,' she said.

They headed to the hospital canteen to buy sparkling water and four blueberry muffins, then went back to the cardiac care unit.

One of the doctors was talking to Mark when they walked into his room.

'Sorry for interrupting. Do you want us to come back later, when you've finished talking to Mum and Dad?' Oliver asked the doctor.

'No, it's fine. I've gone through everything with your parents,' the doctor said. 'By the way, congratulations on your engagement.'

Fizz exchanged a glance with Oliver. This was snowballing already. But she didn't know how to stop it without causing the kind of stress and drama that might be too much for Mark. 'Thank you. We bought healthy bubbles to celebrate,' she said, holding up the bottle of sparkling water, 'and I hope it's OK for Mark to have cake?'

'Of course,' the doctor said with a smile.

'Though he'll be nil by mouth later today, to prepare for tomorrow's operation,' she warned. She looked at Oliver. 'I've given your parents some leaflets and some website links that might help answer any questions—there's a lot to take in—but if you're worried about anything, come and grab one of us and we'll do our best to answer.'

'Thank you,' Oliver said. 'Would you like some sparkling water or cake?'

'I'm afraid I have patients still to see, so I'll have to say no, but thank you for asking,' the doctor said, patting his arm. 'Congratulations again.' She smiled. 'You make a lovely couple.'

'So what happens with the operation?' Oliver asked when the doctor had left the room and they'd all raised a glass of sparkling water to toast the 'engagement'.

'They're going to do an ablation,' Mark said. 'That means they're going to put some wires through my veins, use radio frequencies to take out the electrical pathways that aren't working properly, and then everything should be back to normal and I'll stop feeling so terrible. I'll stay in overnight, and then I can come home.'

'And you have to rest, Mark. The doctor

said he'd be tired for a few days afterwards—weeks, even,' Juliet told Oliver.

'Yes, so *please* don't tell me you're whisking us off to Venice to get married next week,' Mark said, 'because I won't be able to travel.'

Fizz exchanged a glance with Oliver. 'Don't worry, we haven't set a date yet. There's no rush. Just concentrate on getting better, Mark.'

'I suppose you're right,' he said. 'But I'm so glad you're getting married.'

'You need to rest, Dad,' Oliver said. 'I'm going back to the gallery to sort out some things so I can be here tomorrow with Mum during your operation, and then I'll stay with you both and work from your place for the rest of the week, but I'll call in again tonight. Mum, do you want to stay with me, tonight? Or I can come and stay with you, if you'd rather.'

'It'd be nice to have you both at our place,' Juliet said wistfully.

Oliver glanced at Fizz, who nodded. 'I can do that. I'll cook dinner so you don't have to worry about a thing,' she added. 'See you later, Mark. Do what the medics tell you.' She kissed his cheek, and then Juliet's. 'You've got my number, Juliet. Ring me if you need anything at all.'

'Thank you, sweetheart,' Juliet said.

'I can make an excuse if you'd rather not stay at Mum and Dad's tonight,' Oliver said when they were walking out of the hospital towards the Tube. 'And don't worry about dinner. I'll pick up something from the supermarket, or we can get something delivered.'

'It's fine. I think you could both do with the company, and I don't mind cooking,' Fizz said. She paused. 'It looks as if your parents think that we stay over at each other's flats.'

'Well, we do, sometimes, if we've been out somewhere—but not in the way they obviously think we do.' He winced. 'I didn't think about that. Mum will probably assume that, as my fiancée, you'll expect to sleep in my room rather than wanting a guest room. Don't worry, I'll take the floor.'

'And what if she decides to bring us a cup of tea in the morning?' Fizz asked. 'Then we'll have to explain and ask her to keep it secret from your dad, and she doesn't need that kind of stress. Look, we managed in Paris.' Then she remembered waking up in his arms, and how much she'd wanted him; she felt her face heat. This really wasn't appropriate.

'In a month, six weeks tops, we can tell them the truth,' Oliver said.

'We can manage, for now. I'd better start making a replacement for this.' She gestured to the ring on her finger. 'If they notice I'm not wearing it, I can always say I don't wear rings when I'm working, and I forgot to put the ring back on because it's still so new to me.'

'I feel horrible that I'm making you do all that extra work for nothing,' he said.

'It's not a problem. I can use it in publicity material. But we'd better start practising whatever engaged couples do. Hold hands, giggle...'

Just as she hoped, he rolled his eyes. 'I'm not a giggler, and neither are you. For which I am unspeakably glad.'

But he held her hand on the Tube to Camden, and he kissed her lightly on the cheek before she got up—his own stop was three further on the Northern line and then he had a ten-minute walk to the gallery. 'I'll pick you up tonight on my way to the hospital.'

'Ring me before you leave, so I know what time to be ready and outside, waiting for you,' she said.

'Thank you, Fizz. I owe you.'

'No problems. It's what best friends are for,' she said.

Though her head was in a whirl as she walked from the station back to her small flat.

A fake engagement, until Oliver's dad was better. Holding hands and…kissing? Her cheek was still tingling from that little brush of his lips. A full-on kiss on the lips would definitely turn her knees to jelly.

This was probably the worst idea they'd ever had between them.

She shook herself. There was no time to mull it over. She needed to make a replica of the engagement ring she'd just finished, and work out what she was going to cook for dinner for Oliver and his mum, this evening. Gnocchi with caponata sauce, perhaps, a green salad and good bread. That would be quick and easy.

And she wasn't going to let herself think about sharing a bed with Oliver tonight…

A fake engagement.

To Fizz, his best friend. The woman he'd loved for years, always as a friend—once as more than that, but he'd supressed it when he'd realised that she hadn't loved him in the same way.

Was he foolish?

Probably, Oliver thought ruefully. He was worried sick about his parents. Although Fizz had reassured him that his dad was in the right place, he still wondered what would happen if the operation didn't work. Or, even worse, if his dad didn't survive it?

He called a quick staff meeting when he got back to the gallery, explaining that he'd be away tomorrow and working from his parents' house for the next few days. And he had to blink away the stinging in his eyes when Ashley, his father's PA, gave him a 'get well soon' card that everyone in the gallery had signed. 'We'll send him a care package when he's home,' she said. 'Something to keep him occupied. We thought we'd send him a couple of biographies, some good decaf coffee and those biscuits he likes from the Italian deli—if he's allowed them?'

'That would be lovely,' Oliver said. 'Thank you all. It means a lot to know...' The lump in his throat stopped him saying any more.

She patted his arm. 'We know, love. Nobody ever leaves Harrison's Fine Art, except to retire. It's like a family. And it goes without saying that we're here for you, too. If you need any one of us, just call me and I'll sort it out.'

'I really appreciate that,' Oliver said. 'I appreciate all of *you*.'

He sorted out what needed to be done and

when; then he made a couple of phone calls to move meetings, and took a pile of paperwork back to his flat to add to his overnight things. Then he called Fizz. 'I'm leaving my flat in ten minutes.'

'OK. How did it go at the gallery?'

'They all signed a card for Dad. They're planning to send him a care package when he's home. Things to keep him occupied and stop him worrying about work.'

'That's lovely,' Fizz said. 'OK, I'll get my things together. See you soon.'

As he pulled up outside the Victorian terrace where she lived in the ground floor flat, he saw her waiting for him. How ridiculous that his heart did a backflip.

She put her bags in the back of the car and climbed in beside him. 'Any news?'

'I spoke to Mum a few minutes ago and she says Dad's the same as when we left him. He's starting to get a bit nervous about tomorrow.'

'I'm not surprised. How are you holding up?'

'Fine.'

'It's me you're talking to,' she reminded him. 'And I'm not going to say a word to your mum.'

'I'm worried,' he said. 'But you were right when you said he's in the best place.' He took a deep breath. 'And I'm really glad you're going to be here tonight.'

'I'll stay for as long as you need me,' she said. 'I can stay at the hospital with you to-morrow, if that would help.'

'It would help a lot,' he said, and reached across to squeeze her hand briefly.

At the hospital, they stayed for a chat with his father, then drove his mum back to the house in Belsize Park. Juliet went to collect Poppy, the family's Westie, from the next-door neighbour while Fizz busied herself in the kitchen, boiling potatoes to make the gnocchi and chopping ingredients for the sauce, with Oliver helping here and there.

'It feels odd to be here without Dad,' Oliver said.

'He'll be back home, the day after tomorrow,' she reminded him. 'And you can stop scoffing those red peppers or there won't be enough for the sauce.'

'Sorry,' he said.

'Sure you are,' she teased.

How good it felt, having her around.

At dinner, Juliet picked at the gnocchi. 'I'm sorry, love,' she said to Fizz. 'It's not your fault—the food's lovely. I'm just not very hungry.'

'Because you're worried about Mark. Even though you know he's in the best place,' Fizz said. 'Why don't you go and put your feet up, Juliet? I'll make you a mug of chamomile tea and honey.'

'While I clear up in the kitchen,' Oliver said.

'And so you should, as sous-chef,' Fizz said, dropping a kiss on his forehead. It was odd how natural it felt to do something so affectionate.

'You two make such a good team,' Juliet said. 'I did wonder earlier if you were pretending to be engaged, just to keep your dad's spirits up.'

Oliver exchanged a glance with Fizz. Maybe this fake engagement hadn't been his best suggestion. He'd been panicking at the time and it was the first thing he'd thought of. His mum had just given him an opportunity to tell the truth; perhaps he ought to come clean?

But Fizz smiled before he could say anything. 'I love Oli, Juliet. Never doubt that.'

How could he contradict her now?

Sharing a room with her tonight was going to be so awkward.

Except he found it wasn't. Once Fizz had changed into her pyjamas and climbed into bed, she simply patted the mattress beside her. 'Come and talk to me about your favourite painting. It'll take your mind off your worries.'

Weirdly, lying there in the dark with her and talking about art made him feel calmer. As if the world had stopped spinning madly; with Fizz, he felt as if there was a still place, somewhere he could just *be*.

Being here with her felt so right.

Maybe, once his dad was better, he could persuade her to take a chance on him for real...

CHAPTER FIVE

THE NEXT MORNING, Fizz woke first. Oliver looked worn out, so she left him sleeping and went downstairs to let Poppy out. She could hear Juliet moving about upstairs, so she put the kettle on and shook coffee grounds into the cafetiere. Having stayed at Oliver's parents' house before, she knew how Juliet took her coffee and she knew her way round the kitchen well enough to get everything prepped for breakfast.

'Morning,' she said when Juliet came into the kitchen. 'Coffee's just ready.'

'Oh, Fizz, you are a darling. Thank you,' the older woman said gratefully, accepting the mug Fizz handed her. 'I can't believe how lucky we are. You hear all these horror stories about people ending up with the daughter-in-law from hell, and instead we have you—the daughter-in-law we've always wanted. You're perfect for Oliver.'

'I have my faults, you know,' Fizz said. 'I'm impulsive and I can go off into a daydream. Ask Oli how many times he has to tell me to pay attention when he's talking to me.'

Juliet chuckled. 'You're a breath of fresh air, love.'

Fizz inclined her head and smiled in acknowledgement of the compliment. 'How's Mark this morning? I assume you've already called him.'

'I have. He's nervous. And hungry,' Juliet said.

'Ah. If he's like Oli in the morning, he needs coffee and carbs before you can even speak to him.'

'Like father, like son,' Juliet agreed.

'I'll go and prod Oli awake,' Fizz said. 'The toast will be ready in a moment. Oh, and I let Poppy out earlier.'

The Westie, hearing her name, wagged her tail, but sat where she was with her gaze fixed on Juliet, waiting for her share of toast crusts.

'Thank you,' Juliet said.

Oliver, predictably, grunted at her when she tried to wake him. She ignored him. 'Breakfast is ready downstairs. Go and join your mum while I have a shower.'

Oliver grumbled, but hauled himself out of bed and headed down to the kitchen.

Fizz smiled to herself. For a moment, she could see herself in twenty years' time, with a grumpy husband and an equally grumpy teenage son, neither of whom were fit for conversation until they'd had breakfast, and a daughter who was wide awake and teasing them both.

She shook herself. Where on earth had that come from? Apart from the fact that her engagement to Oliver was completely fake, she'd never thought about having children. Well. Not since those weeks after Laura's death, when everything was grim and she was full of panic about what her future held. When she'd walked for miles and miles, but nothing had been able to clear her head or help her decide what to do.

She tamped it down, determined not to dwell on it as she finished showering and changing. Knowing that it was going to be a very long day with a lot of waiting around, she'd brought playing cards and a travel Scrabble from her flat to take to the hospital. Even if they were reduced to playing Snap because they couldn't concentrate on anything more complicated, it would at least be a distraction.

'I'll take Poppy for her w-a-l-k while you get dressed, Juliet,' she said, spelling out the word so the little Westie didn't get overexcited.

'Thank you, love.'

'Are you human yet, Oli?' she teased, kissing him on the cheek. Warmth bloomed in her chest when he leaned into her. She knew they needed these little moments of affection if they were going to keep up their ruse until Mark was better. But she hadn't expected them to play havoc with her real emotions too.

'Nearly,' he grouched. Poppy woofed, and Oli sighed. 'All right. Sit, paw, and then you can have this crust.'

Poppy sat obediently with a paw raised, and deftly caught the bit of toast that Oliver threw to her. Fizz attached the lead to Poppy's collar. 'See you in a bit.'

By the time she got back with Poppy, Juliet and Oliver were ready to go to the hospital. Juliet took the Westie to her neighbour's house, and then Oliver drove them in. Mark was delighted to see them all. Although Fizz could see that he had the same tension 'tell' as Oliver did—a tightening around his eyes—

he hid his nervousness with a stream of terrible dad jokes until he had to say goodbye to Juliet at the door to the operating theatre.

Fizz was very aware of Oliver's worries about whether his father would survive the operation, and she was pretty sure that Juliet thought the same, even though she hadn't voiced them to Fizz. Both of them were surreptitiously looking at their watches every couple of minutes, and the hours seemed to go by so very slowly. But somehow she kept them going throughout the operation, playing games, making sure they were drinking water and eating properly.

Finally one of the nursing team came into the relatives' room to see them. 'I'm pleased to say Mark's come round from the anaesthetic and is properly awake now,' she said. 'The ablation looks as if it's been successful, and you can go in to see him. Though he must keep lying flat for the next few hours.'

'Thank you.' Juliet was almost in tears with relief.

Oliver's voice sounded equally wobbly as he thanked the nurse; he held Fizz's hand tightly as he followed his mother out of the waiting room and into his father's room.

'They're letting me home tomorrow,' Mark said, 'but there are so many rules. No driving, no lifting or strenuous exercise, no alcohol, *still* no coffee...and I have to lie flat for the rest of the afternoon.' He rolled his eyes. 'It's going to drive me mad.'

'You follow every single one of those rules to the letter, Mark Harrison,' Juliet said fiercely, 'because I don't want to be without you for a single second more than I have to.'

'I don't want to be without you, either, Jools,' Mark said.

Fizz swallowed the lump in her throat and glanced at Oliver, who was looking straight at her. What would it be like to have someone feel that way about her?

She realised that was the way she felt about Oliver. It wasn't just uncomplicated friendship, any more. It was turning into something else, something she hadn't expected. Or was this whole fake fiancée thing just messing with her head?

'We'll let you rest, Dad,' Oliver said. 'Mum, I'll come and pick you up later.'

'I've got client appointments first thing tomorrow,' Fizz said, 'so I'm going back home tonight, Juliet, but if you need anything just ring me. And I'll come over tomorrow evening to see you—let me know if you need anything from the shop.'

'You're such a sweetheart, Fizz,' Mark said, squeezing her hand. 'I'm so glad you're officially going to be part of our family.'

What could she do but smile and say, 'So am I.'

Oliver insisted on driving Fizz back to his parents' house and then, once she'd collected her bags, dropping her back at her flat.

'Thank you for everything you've done.' He held her tightly. 'I'll call you tomorrow.'

Now wasn't the time to tell him of her misgivings about them getting in too deep with this fake engagement thing, Fizz thought. Or how she was starting to feel about him. Right now, he was as vulnerable as she'd been the night they'd ended up kissing—and she understood now why he'd called a halt. 'All right. And call me if you can't sleep,' she said instead.

He didn't call her. She got through her meetings the next morning and then spent the rest of the day working on the fake engagement ring. In the middle of the afternoon, her doorbell rang. Odd: she wasn't expecting a delivery, and she knew Oliver was in Belsize Park, taking care of his parents.

She was taken aback by the gorgeous arrangement of white roses, stocks and delphiniums. 'Are you sure they're for me?' she asked the driver.

'If you're Felicity Bennett, yes,' he said.

She put the flowers on the table and opened the card that came with it.

Congratulations on your engagement to Oliver, with love from all at Harrison's Fine Art.

Oh, no.

How had his company found out? This engagement business was starting to get out of control, and she didn't know how to calm things down.

She called Oliver.

'Everything OK?' he asked.

'Uh-huh. Are your parents nearby?'

'In the living room.'

'Go upstairs, and video-call me back with the door closed.'

'All right.' He sounded surprised, but hung up and then video-called her a couple of minutes later. 'What's wrong?'

'I just got these.' She moved the screen briefly so he could see the flowers.

'Very flashy. Who are they from?'

'All the team at Harrison's Fine Art. Congratulating me on our engagement.'

He blew out a breath. 'Ah. Ashley—Dad's PA—popped in to see him this afternoon, with a care package from the team. He must have told her the news. And she must've sorted out the flowers locally, since you got them that fast.'

'What are we going to do, Oli?' she asked. 'We can't keep lying to the whole world.'

'I know, but Dad's going to take a few weeks to recover.' He grimaced.

She sighed. 'All right. I'll send a thank-you card to the gallery tomorrow. And I'll send an excited photo to you and your parents.'

'Actually, I was going to call you anyway—Mum wanted to invite you to dinner tonight.'

Did he want her to make an excuse? Or did he need the moral support? She didn't have a clue, so she asked him outright.

'Both,' he said. 'I'll make an excuse because it's not fair to lean on you. I'm old enough to handle this stuff myself.'

'I'll be there,' she said. 'Princess Fizz to the rescue.'

To her relief, he laughed. 'I thought the princes were supposed to be the rescuers?'

'Nope. Princesses can do—'

'—anything princes can do,' he finished, 'particularly because you're one of the Bennett sisters, which gives you extra superpowers. OK. Does half-past seven work for you?'

'It does,' she said. 'See you then.'

She ended the call, and sat staring at the ring on her desk. This whole thing had started with a mistake, and then continued with the best of intentions. But she hadn't thought about it spreading further than his parents. Right now it seemed in danger of getting out of control.

Maybe Darcy would have a good idea how to fix this.

Fizz rang her sister, but Darcy didn't answer her phone.

This wasn't something she wanted to talk about by text. Maybe some fresh air would sort her head out. She went out to the shops; on the way to the florists, she noticed a new display in the bookshop on the corner. There was a book of historical-based puzzles. It was the sort of thing Mark would enjoy, and it might keep him occupied and sitting still, she thought, rather than being restless and worrying Juliet. She went inside to buy a copy, then picked up the rest of the things on her list before heading back to her flat and making the collets for the smaller gems on the outside of the ring.

The alarm on her phone warned her when it was time to pack everything away on her jeweller's bench. Armed with the book for Mark, some roses for Juliet, dog treats for Poppy and a tub of Oliver's favourite artisan ice cream from the deli on her road, she caught the Tube to Belsize Park.

Juliet was thrilled with the roses, Mark loved the book, Poppy wagged her tail madly at the crinkle of the bag of treats, and Oliver kissed her. On the lips. 'Best treat ever,' he said. 'Dad fancied something Indian for dinner, so I've made the heart-healthy version—plain rice, tandoori chicken, dhal and veggie dhansak.' He smiled. 'Go and sit down. I'll bring everything in.'

Fizz headed to the table, her lips still tingling from Oliver's kiss. Was he as affected as she was? He didn't seem to be. She needed to get her head on straight and remind herself this was for show. Oliver was just playing the part and she needed to do the same—for her friend's sake. Real emotions had no place here.

She made the effort to pull herself together. She couldn't risk their friendship, not when she couldn't give Oliver what he really deserved— she was too broken. But she could be there for her *friend*.

The food was wonderful, perfectly cooked and full of flavour.

'Did you get the photograph I sent you of the flowers from the gallery, Mark?' Fizz asked. 'They were so gorgeous.'

Mark looked pleased. 'I hope you don't mind that I told Ashley. My staff at the gallery are more like family anyway, and they wanted to celebrate with you and Oliver.'

Fizz felt a flush of guilt at the fib she and Oliver were telling—but it was in a good cause, she reminded herself. The best cause.

'And, what with everything that's happened, we haven't asked you about Paris,' Juliet said. 'Where did Oliver propose to you?'

Help. How did she answer that?

To her relief, Oliver swept in. 'By the clock in the Musée d'Orsay. It's the perfect place,' he said.

'What did your parents say when you told them?' Mark asked. 'And your sister must be thrilled at the idea of being a bridesmaid.'

Fizz shuffled in her seat. 'I haven't told them yet.' At Mark's look of concern, she added quietly, 'They're still in Provence. It was Laura's anniversary a few days ago. They need some quiet time before they'll have the headspace to celebrate.'

'Oh, of course,' Juliet said. 'I'm sorry, love. You must miss your sister.'

'Hugely,' Fizz said.

'And your oldest sister lives somewhere up north, doesn't she?' Mark asked.

'Edinburgh,' Fizz said. 'She fell in love with the place after university.' It was true, up to a point. Although she knew they'd assume Darcy had been a student there, it was better to tell the small fib than to give them the whole horrible story about how Darcy had fled there after Damian dumped her at the altar.

'I'll clear the table,' Mark said, standing up.

Fizz noticed that he was still a bit breathless. 'Sit down, Mark. You're meant to be resting. I'll do this—and I count as family rather than a guest, now, so it's OK for me to help out,' she said.

'I suppose you're right,' Mark said. He frowned. 'But I do feel a bit like a spare part.'

'Dad, you had a four-hour operation yesterday,' Oliver reminded him. 'The surgeon said that you need to pace yourself. You're not a spare part at all—and we want you around for a *lot* longer. I know it's frustrating for you, but can you please just do what they told you and rest?'

Mark nodded. 'Still, at least we have a wedding to plan.'

'That's mine and Fizz's job,' Oliver cut in swiftly, to her relief. 'We're still thinking about what we want.'

'But you've known each other for nearly a decade!'

'Bit of an exaggeration, Dad,' Oliver said mildly.

'I just hope you don't take as long to decide where you'll get married as you did to get engaged in the first place,' Mark grumbled.

'We won't,' Fizz said with the sweetest of smiles.

'Let's see the ring again,' Juliet said.

Fizz winced. 'Sorry, Juliet—it's back at my flat. I was working earlier, and I never wear anything on my hands or wrists when I'm working. It's still so new that I forgot to put it back on my finger.'

Juliet looked disappointed. 'Oh, well. Another time.'

'Another time,' Fizz promised.

After they'd cleared up in the kitchen, played a board game and Mark had finally admitted that perhaps he could do with an early night, Oliver drove Fizz home.

'Your parents will expect you to dally a bit,' Fizz said, 'so you might as well come in for a drink. Chamomile tea?'

Oliver groaned. 'Is this my fiancée trying to reform my coffee habit?'

She laughed. 'I thought I'd try it on. All right, I'll make you coffee.'

She was just pouring hot water into the mugs when her phone pinged. Glancing at the screen, she saw that finally Darcy was returning her call.

Well, not actually *calling* her. Instead, her sister had sent a selfie from the Colosseum. Standing next to her was a good-looking dark-haired man Fizz had never seen before. The only words with the photo were Loving Rome.

What?

OK, Laura had told them to go and have a wild twenty-four hours; and the guy was gorgeous. Darcy was more than overdue some fun. But what worried Fizz most was that her sister looked starry-eyed.

She sent Darcy a barrage of questions.

Who is he?

How long have you known him?

How are you? How's Rome?

And Darcy didn't answer a single one.

'I recognise that frown,' Oliver said. 'What's up?'

'Darcy. I'm worried about her. She's doing her bucket list city trip.'

'Darcy will be fine,' Oliver said. 'She's the oldest, and she's used to doing things her way. She can look after herself.'

'I still worry about who this guy is next to her.' She showed him the photo. 'I don't even know his name. And she didn't tell me she was going to Rome. She only said it was a maybe on her list.'

'Did you tell her you were going to Paris, before we went?'

'Yes. And I sent photos to her, Mum and Dad while I was there. You took some of the photos for me,' she reminded him.

'Perhaps she forgot to tell you because she was being spontaneous,' Oliver suggested.

'You mean, Laura meant she should be more Fizz?' she asked wryly. 'And I should be more Darcy. She's on her second task, and I haven't even thought about which one I'm going to do next. Laura wanted us to do it all within six weeks, and at this rate I'm going to end up panicking and doing everything else on the very last day.'

'I kind of derailed you because of Dad, so I'll help you.' He paused. 'Have you told Darcy about our, um, "engagement"?'

'No. I was going to, but she hasn't returned my calls. She just sent me this instead.' She stared at the photograph. 'It's obvious that she's busy.'

'This is Darcy we're talking about. She's not going to do anything rash,' Oliver said. 'Chill. What are you going to do next on Laura's list?'

She had three things left. Commitment, facing a fear, and taking time to think. It was becoming clearer to her now that thinking should be the last thing on the list, the thing that would help her ease into the rest of her life. Facing her fear… No, not yet. Which left her with one thing. 'Making a commitment,' she said. 'I don't suppose a fake engagement would count?'

'No, it wouldn't.' Oliver gave her a wry smile.

'Laura said it has to be something important. I would consider adopting a dog—I think, from what Darcy's said, that's what she's going to do—but my flat's completely the wrong environment for a dog.'

'It doesn't have to be a pet,' Oliver said. 'What about committing to something that will connect you to people?'

'Such as?'

'Joining a choir?' he suggested.

'Not with my flat singing,' she said wryly. 'Once they'd heard me, they'd politely suggest that I stuck to being their biscuit monitor or something.'

'Mentoring a young jeweller? Teaching a class once a week? Volunteering?'

'I'll have a think about it,' she said. 'Sorry, I don't mean to shut you down—you've actually been really helpful because you're making me think about what I can do.' She hugged him. It was the same hug she'd given him a thousand times. And yet, something about it felt different. It wasn't like their old, easy friendship. There was something else, something she couldn't quite put her finger on. Something that scared her and thrilled her at the same time.

He kissed the top of her head. 'Any time.'

She knew he meant it. He'd always been there for her. But what if things changed while they were pretending to be more? Would he still be her friend then?

CHAPTER SIX

THE NEXT DAY, Fizz went out to pick up some milk and spied a gorgeous red jug with white polka dots in the window of the charity shop next to the supermarket.

When she paid for it, she noticed the ginger cat sitting on a cushion in a patch of sunlight. 'What a gorgeous cat,' she said to the woman at the cash desk. 'Can I make a fuss of them, or would they rather be left alone?'

'She'd enjoy the fuss. Her name's Tilly,' the cashier said.

'Hello, Tilly.' Fizz held out her hand, and the cat rubbed her face against it to signal acceptance. Fizz stroked her, and the cat purred.

'Is she yours?' Fizz asked.

'Yes and no. It's tricky.' The cashier bit her lip. 'Tilly's actually my neighbour's cat. I promised to look after her while he was in hospital—except he died, last week.'

'Oh, dear. I'm sorry,' Fizz said.

'He was a nice old man. Sadly, he didn't have any family, so there isn't anyone who could take her in. I'm looking after her for the moment, but I can't keep her because my partner has asthma and since Tilly's been staying with us he's been struggling quite a bit.' The cashier sighed. 'I know I ought to take her to the rescue centre down the road, but I just haven't been able to bring myself to do it yet. She's thirteen, and people tend to prefer kittens who'll play for hours to elderly cats who just want a quiet life. It might be a long time before they can find someone suitable, and I don't think she'd enjoy being in a rescue centre. She's used to a home.' She shook her head. 'I've been bringing her here during the day and crossing my fingers that the area manager won't turn up unexpectedly and tell me I can't keep her here.'

'Why would he do that?' Fizz asked. 'Surely all the customers like her?'

'Yes, and she's no trouble—all she wants is a patch of sunlight to snooze in and the odd cuddle—but he's a bit of a stickler for regulations,' the cashier said. 'If there's a health and safety issue, he'll bring it up in the first five seconds.'

In Fizz's student days, her landlady had

lived on the top floor of their house and had a cat who used to enjoy spending time with the students. On nights in, Fizz had enjoyed curling up on the sofa with Bubbles the calico cat snoozing on her lap.

This was an absurd idea.

But, if it worked, she'd be making a commitment that would benefit someone else. Doing something important. Giving an elderly cat a comfortable, happy home for the rest of her days.

'I know I'm a stranger, and of course you're not going to give a cat to just anyone, but maybe I could give her a home,' Fizz said. 'If we get the rescue centre involved, then Tilly gets a proper safeguard. Maybe someone could foster her—or maybe you could keep her for a few more days—just until the rescue centre has a meeting with me and decides whether I'm a suitable owner.'

'Maybe,' the cashier said, looking doubtful.

'I work from home, so Tilly would have company all day, most of the time,' Fizz added. 'Guaranteed cuddles and a comfy bed.'

Tilly looked up from her cushion and miaowed softly, as if she knew they were talking about her.

'Give me your number, and I'll talk to my partner tonight,' the cashier said. 'I'm Trisha, by the way.'

'Felicity, but everyone calls me Fizz,' Fizz said, shaking her hand.

They exchanged phone numbers, and Fizz sent Trisha the link to her website and social media accounts. 'You can look me up, just to reassure yourself and the rescue centre that I'm not some random weird person,' she said.

Tilly miaowed again, as if in agreement.

'All right. I'll be in touch,' Trisha said.

Fizz's bride-to-be was thrilled with the sunflower ring when Fizz dropped it off at her office at lunchtime. 'It's absolutely perfect,' she said, nudging her fiancé. 'I'm just going to smile and smile every time I look at it.'

He stowed it safely in his pocket. 'I can't wait for you to be officially my fiancée, Aleisha.'

'And the engagement's tomorrow night?' Fizz asked.

'The party's tomorrow night,' Aleisha said. 'But we're getting engaged tomorrow morning. Just the two of us.'

'As soon as the National Gallery opens,' her fiancé said. 'When it'll still be quiet. And I'm going to ask her to marry me in front of her favourite painting in the world.'

'Van Gogh's *Sunflowers*,' Aleisha said. 'And obviously I'm going to say yes. We're going to ask the gallery staff to take a picture—not for social media, but for *us*.'

'That's lovely. I'm sure they'll help. I wish you both every happiness,' Fizz said, smiling. 'And it's been a privilege to make this for you.' Even if it had ended up landing her in a situation she really hadn't expected.

She headed back home and worked on the silver and zircona replica, soldering the collets to the ring. What would it be like if she and Oliver were engaged for real? Would he think of somewhere special to propose and slide the ring onto her finger? Stupid question: of course he would. Except he wasn't going to propose to her for real, and this whole thing was messing with her head.

She was still thinking about Oliver when he called her. 'Are you busy tonight?'

'I don't have anything planned,' she admitted. 'Why?'

'Would you like to come to the theatre with me? My parents had tickets for the first night of *A Midsummer Night's Dream* in Covent Garden, but Dad doesn't feel quite up to it and

Mum doesn't want to leave him home alone, so she's offered us their tickets.'

'Yes, please—that's my favourite Shakespeare,' Fizz said. 'Can I get a nice dinner delivered to your parents in return?'

'Way ahead of you. I've already booked it,' he said. 'I've got a meeting at the gallery, this afternoon. I know we'll both be going in on the Northern Line, but I think it's probably easier if we meet outside Leicester Square Tube station.'

It was a sensible suggestion; in the rush hour of commuters, they wouldn't have a hope of finding each other on the platform at Goodge Street, the closest station to the gallery, let alone on the Tube itself. 'OK. What time?'

'Quarter to six,' he said. 'Because we've also got Mum and Dad's reservation for a pre-theatre dinner in Covent Garden. We'll walk there from Leicester Square, and I'll buy you dinner.'

'Thank you—that'd be great,' she said. 'See you later.'

She set an alarm on her phone to make sure she had enough time to get ready before the theatre, and continued working on the ring, gradually sanding down the silver to perfect smoothness.

When her alarm buzzed, she chose her favourite little black dress—a V-necked crepe slip dress with spaghetti straps—and teamed it with a silver and enamel sunflower choker on a black velvet ribbon, a sunflower silver and enamel bracelet, and red court shoes that looked like killer heels but were actually really comfortable to walk in. She left her hair loose and wore the minimum of make-up, just enough to emphasise her lips and her eyelashes.

Oliver was already waiting when she arrived at Leicester Square—dead on time.

'You look stunning,' he said.

She inclined her head in acknowledgement of the compliment. 'You don't scrub up too badly yourself,' she said. He was wearing a navy suit with a crisp white shirt and an understated tie, clearly his office suit. 'Good meeting?'

'Very,' he said, and tucked her arm through his.

At the restaurant, they chose different mains and starters, so they could taste each other's; it was a joy having a best friend who liked food as much as she did, and liked trying new things. She swapped a mouthful of her bruschetta with cannellini beans and pancetta for his agrodolce summer squash, and a taste of her gnocchi with chicken and chilli pesto for his risotto primavera. They finished with cheese, fennel crackers and fig jam, washed down with a good Venetian valpolicella.

'The food here is fantastic,' Oliver said, leaning back against his chair with a sigh of pleasure. 'We'll have to come back here.'

'Definitely,' she said. 'Next time, it's my treat.'

Somehow they ended up walking with their arms round each other between the restaurant and the theatre, and Oliver held her hand throughout the play. They were just practising for their public role as an engaged couple, she told herself; though it felt surprisingly good to sit beside him with his fingers tangled with hers. She actually felt a tingle in her knees, as if they'd gone all weak on her—something she hadn't expected to happen with Oliver.

Then again, since Paris, everything had felt different. It had changed her awareness of him; had it changed his awareness of her?

He held her hand when they left the theatre, too. Neither of them commented on it, and she kept the conversation light all the way back to Camden, chatting about the play.

'I really regret not being part of the drama society, as a student,' she said. 'They did *A Midsummer Night's Dream* in my last year, and I would've loved to play Puck.'

'Because of his impetuous streak?' Oliver teased.

'Because he gets to fix things when they go wrong,' she corrected.

'But they go wrong in the first place because of him,' Oliver said. 'Plus Oberon didn't actually order him to turn Bottom into an ass. Puck did that himself, out of pure mischief.'

She grinned. 'But we all know someone like Bottom—someone who's just too much and needs taking down a peg or two. Wouldn't it be fun to be able to give them an ass's head for a day? Though my absolute favourite bit in the play is when the Mechanicals perform Pyramus and Thisbe. Written down, it's dull. On stage, it's *hilarious*.' She raised an eyebrow. 'Who would you be?'

He laughed. 'Oberon, so I could boss everyone around.'

'That's so not you,' she said, shaking her head. 'Oberon's a bully. He's the epitome of the malevolent fae. I'd design him a crown of spikes and tangles, all shadowy and sharp.'

'All right. Who do *you* think I'd be, then?' he asked.

'Peter Quince,' she said.

He raised an eyebrow. 'Ambitious but lacking talent?'

'Not at all,' she said. 'You're clear-sighted and you direct people for the good of the company. You know your team, you know what they're good at, and you can see where they'd get something out of being stretched.'

'That,' he said, 'is a lovely thing to say. And it's how I want to run Harrison's. Like Dad did, but maybe broadening things out a bit.'

'And that,' she said, 'is why he picked the perfect person to take over from him.'

He squeezed her hand. 'Thank you.'

Oliver got off at her Tube stop so he could walk her back to her flat.

'Do you want to come in for a glass of wine?' she asked.

'That'd be nice,' he said.

She connected her phone to her speaker in the living room and found some slow blues they both liked on her streaming service. Then she pulled the curtains, switched on a lamp, poured them both a glass of red and sat on the sofa next to him.

'My bride-to-be and her fiancé picked up their sunflower ring today.' She smiled. 'It's so romantic. They're getting officially engaged tomorrow morning as soon as the National Gallery's open, in front of the *Sunflowers* because it's her favourite painting in the world. Well, that's why they chose me as their designer, because she's already got some of my earrings and loves them.'

'That's special,' he agreed. 'Something they'll always remember.'

She took a deep breath. 'I'm sorry I've deprived you of a proper engagement.'

'You mean our fake one at the Musée d'Orsay, with no pictures?' he asked. 'That's not a big deal.'

Wasn't it? 'Your mum and dad must think it's odd, though,' she mused. 'That we didn't even take a photograph of something so momentous, I mean.'

'We could always have a quiet private engagement when you've finished making the replica ring,' he said.

'That'll be tomorrow. Though, actually, I have plans for tomorrow—with any luck, it's my next bucket list thing. Commitment.'

He looked intrigued. 'What did you decide to go for in the end? Mentoring or teaching?'

'Neither,' she said. 'It's the weirdest coincidence. I went out for some milk and I saw this jug I really liked in the window of the charity shop round the corner.' She told him about the ginger cat and what she'd learned of Tilly's plight. 'Trisha's talking it over with her partner. Hopefully she'll be happy for me to take Tilly, and then we'll go to the cat rescue place and formalise me adopting Tilly. That way everyone gets a safeguard and everybody wins. And I'm fulfilling Laura's list— because it's a commitment, it's long term, and I'll be making a difference to the life of an elderly cat who's just lost her owner.'

'Didn't the landlady in your second-year digs have a cat who spent a lot of her time draped round your neck?' he asked. 'A pretty cat, black and white and ginger.'

'Bubbles,' she confirmed. 'She liked cuddles. Obviously it's hard to sketch with a cat on your lap, and that's why she ended up draped round my neck so often. The art student's answer to a pirate's parrot,' she added with a grin. 'Actually, I think I'd like to have a cat. She'd fit into my lifestyle without me worrying about getting her enough exercise, as I would with a dog. Keep your fingers crossed for me that I can adopt Tilly.'

'I will. I have to admit, that's one of the things I've enjoyed about staying with my parents to keep an eye on them, this week— it's been nice having a dog around,' he said.

'Poppy's a sweetheart,' she agreed. 'I was thinking: if your dad's feeling up to it, the weather's meant to be nice on Sunday. Maybe we could take your parents for a gentle walk round the garden of a stately home, and I can treat them to afternoon tea as a thank you for the theatre tickets.'

'I'll ask them tomorrow and let you know,' he said. He finished his wine and stood up. 'Thanks for the wine. Keep me posted on your commitment situation tomorrow.'

'I will,' she said. Part of her was tempted to ask him to join her; though she didn't want to put pressure on him. He had enough on his plate, worrying about his parents. 'Thanks for this evening, Oli. I had a really lovely time.'

'Me, too.' He bent his head to kiss her cheek, and somehow his lips ended up brushing the corner of her mouth. She wasn't sure which of them turned their head—maybe both of them—but then they were really kissing, his arms wrapped round her and holding her close, and her hands in his hair and urging him on.

Everything around them was forgotten. The soft lights, the music, whatever they'd been talking about—everything vanished in the whirlwind of that kiss.

When he finally pulled away from her, both of them were shaking. His pupils were so huge that his eyes looked black. And he looked as dazed as she felt.

'That wasn't…'

'I didn't…'

They both stopped, not wanting to talk over each other.

'That wasn't meant to happen,' he said. 'Sorry.'

'My fault completely,' she said. 'Sorry.'

And she could see he knew she wasn't sorry at all—just as she knew he wasn't, either.

This had been going to happen ever since Paris. Ever since they'd danced together by the side of the Seine and she'd thought he was going to kiss her then. Ever since they'd agreed on this ridiculous fake engagement. And especially ever since they'd wandered through Covent Garden this evening, holding hands.

But what now? If they turned their fake engagement into a real relationship, what if everything went wrong? She didn't want to lose him from her life. But at the same time she knew they couldn't stay like this, either.

Was he panicking about this as much as she was?

But he seemed to get his head together more quickly than she did.

'We need to talk,' he said. 'But not right now, when we're both a bit shell-shocked. Maybe tomorrow.'

'When we've had time to think everything through,' she agreed.

'Goodnight,' he said, and this time he didn't kiss her, not even on the cheek. Which was probably just as well, even though at the same time it made her feel miserable.

Knowing she was being a coward in not facing up to the situation, Fizz spent Saturday morning immersed in work, and at lunchtime she had a call from Trisha. 'I've spoken to the rescue centre. If you're free on Monday lunchtime, we can go together and sort out the paperwork.'

'That's wonderful news,' she said. 'Thank you. And I should add that you're always welcome to pop round and see her any time.'

She sent a text to Oliver.

Busy working today. Seeing rescue centre people about Tilly on Monday.

He texted back.

Good news.

The ball appeared to be very much in her court. Well, she'd just leave it there for now, because she wasn't ready to talk about that kiss.

Did you ask your parents about tomorrow?

Yes. Can they decide tomorrow?

Of course—if your dad doesn't feel up to it, I understand. Will wait to hear from you.

On Sunday morning, Oliver texted her.

Sorry. Dad's still feeling a bit rough. Maybe next Sunday?

Absolutely, she responded. Give your parents my love.

Will do. Let me know how you get on with the rescue centre.

He'd let her off the hook; it gave her another couple of days' breathing space to decide how to react to that kiss. How to react to him. And what she was going to do next.

On Monday, Fizz saw the rescue centre people, who wanted to visit her flat before they made the final decision.

On Tuesday morning, she made sure she had good biscuits to offer with the tea and coffee, and gave Nadira, the assessor, a tour of her flat.

'I thought Tilly could have a bed in my bedroom as well as a bed in the living room,' she said. 'Plus a litter tray in the bathroom, and her water bowl and food bowl in the kitchen. Trisha told me she's an indoor cat, and she's used to company because her previous owner was elderly; I work from home, so she'll have me around most of the time.' She gestured to the jeweller's bench and worktop in her living room. 'Not that much of my work is noisy— for those bits, maybe she can go and nap in my bedroom.'

Nadira made notes. 'That's good. She'll need a snug place to hide away while she settles in. It can be an igloo-type bed or even just a cardboard box with holes cut into it and a blanket inside.'

Fizz smiled. 'Trisha has Tilly's bed from her previous home, so that should help her settle in. I'll get her a second bed, and I'll keep her with the same vet so she has continuity of care.'

'I think this is going to be a good home for her,' Nadira said. 'Congratulations.' She was able to give advice on which food to get, and how to help Tilly to settle in with a cat pheromone spray. 'If you don't have a carrier from her previous owner, you'll need a carrier when you pick her up.'

Fizz nodded. 'I'm going to check things with Trisha, then head to the pet shop. I'll get her a scratching post and some toys, too.'

'Sounds perfect,' Nadira said with a smile.

On Wednesday, Fizz called in on Trisha to pick up Tilly, brought the cat back to her flat, and in a ridiculously short space of time Tilly had investigated the flat, decided on her favourite spot in the living room, and was happily snoozing in a patch of sunlight.

Unable to resist the impulse, she took a photograph and sent it to Oliver.

Tilly says hello and would you like to come and meet her tonight?

The reply was almost immediate.

Love to. What time?

Seven? Thought we could order a Chinese take-away. Usual?

Yes, please. See you then.

Next, she sent the pic to Darcy.

My name's Tilly, I love sleeping in the sun, and I live with your sister as of today.

To her relief, Darcy responded quickly.

OMG! You got a rescue cat?

Sort of. She's elderly and her owner died. We made friends in the charity shop where she was staying temporarily. Tilly's my commitment.

She's gorgeous.

A picture of a fox-red Labrador appeared on Fizz's screen.

I might have a new friend, too. Going back for a second visit at the weekend.

A dog would really suit Darcy, Fizz thought.

That's lovely!

She was itching to know if there was any more news about the guy in the photo, but she didn't want to make her sister back off.

Everything going OK? she asked instead, giving Darcy the opportunity to tell her more.

Yep. You?

No, it wasn't. It was getting complicated. And Fizz was fully aware that she was using Tilly as an excuse not to have the discussion with Oliver about that kiss.

Yep, she fibbed.

At seven precisely, her doorbell rang. Oliver came in with a brown paper bag. 'I brought a couple of housewarming gifts for Tilly.'

They turned out to be a catnip mouse and a 'fishing rod' toy with a feathery bundle on the end. Tilly loved them. She also took to Oliver immediately, sitting on his lap and purring loudly.

'I think she's just taken over chairmanship of your fan club,' Fizz said with a grin.

'It's mutual. She's lovely,' he said, smiling back.

And their mutual admiration of her new commitment made things much easier for her to manage. She could still avoid talking about that kiss. She wasn't going to bring up the subject unless he did.

A few minutes later, their Chinese food arrived. She'd already put bowls and cutlery on the small bistro table in her kitchen, and she slotted the cartons in the spaces between them with extra spoons for serving. 'Kung Pao chicken, veggie chow mein, crispy duck with pancakes, and mushroom fried rice.' She took a bottle of soy sauce from the cupboard.

'It smells wonderful,' he said.

Tilly looked hopeful and gave a single plaintive miaow when Oliver shredded the crispy duck for the pancakes, but Fizz shook her head. 'Sorry, puss. The spice and sauces aren't good for you. But I did buy a bit of cold poached salmon yesterday to help you settle

in. You can have some of that while we eat.'
She went to the fridge to get the salmon and
chopped it up in Tilly's bowl.

'I think you've fallen on all four paws
here, Tilly,' Oliver said, rubbing the top of
the cat's head.

'She's helping me, too,' Fizz said. 'If it
wasn't for her, I'd still be a bit stuck on task
two of the bucket list.' She put the cat's bowl
on the floor and Tilly ate daintily.

'Halfway there. So that leaves doing something that scares you and thinking about what
you want,' Oliver said.

Her eyes caught his. She was beginning to
think that the two things were actually one
and the same; she certainly couldn't have one
without the other. 'I still have a bit of time,'
she said.

At the weekend, Mark was feeling a lot
more himself, so Fizz and Oliver found a
seventeenth-century house with a gorgeous
walled garden and plenty of seating where
he and Juliet could have a gentle stroll to
enjoy the late spring flowers and stop for
a rest whenever Mark needed to. Fizz took
photographs of flowers that she thought had

potential for a jewellery collection, and Oliver found a wisteria tunnel.

'To inspire your seed pearl earrings,' he said.

'Oh, yes. And you can look decorative for me.' She grinned, and took various shots of Oliver with the wisteria in the background.

'Mum and Dad are coming,' he murmured. 'So I'm going to kiss you, OK?'

The warning wasn't quite enough to stop her knees turning to jelly when he rested his hands on her waist and brushed his mouth against hers. His sunglasses hid his eyes, so she couldn't tell if the kiss had had the same effect on him as it had on her.

'Oh, you two,' Juliet sighed, clearly delighted to have caught them kissing. 'What it is to be young.'

'I can still kiss my wife,' Mark said, proving it. 'And hold her hand.'

'Let me take a picture of you together,' Fizz said, and snapped away. 'I'll Bluetooth them across to you over tea.'

Juliet produced her phone from her bag. 'Let me take a picture of you together, too.'

Oliver draped his arm casually round her shoulders, and her skin tingled where his bare arm touched hers. Though she had a feeling that even if she'd worn a thick coat instead of a strappy summery dress, and he'd had long sleeves instead of a T-shirt, she would still have been just as aware of him.

What was she going to do about this?

The question ticked round and round her brain as they headed for the café and found a table for a full-blown afternoon tea. Trying to push it into the background, she smiled and laughed at Juliet's anecdotes of Oliver as a toddler. But she was very aware of Oliver's arm across the back of her chair, and how easy it would be to shuffle her chair just that little bit closer and lean into him.

Today was meant to be an afternoon out to give Mark a change of scenery and Juliet a bit of a break. And it was working; the strain had lessened on both their faces.

But it was also crystallising for Fizz what she wanted.

A partner with a family background like her own, close and loving.

Scratch that. What she wanted was Oliver. But.

How did she know this wasn't going to go wrong? She'd never told anyone about that awful night, five years ago. She'd tried to keep it boxed in and shut away, so it wouldn't hurt anyone else.

If she told him what she'd done, would he think less of her? Would he change his mind about her?

The longer you kept a secret, the more dangerous it became.

And she had a nasty feeling this could all blow apart.

CHAPTER SEVEN

'YOU'RE LOOKING WORRIED,' Oliver said, when she met him for a drink in the middle of the week. 'Spill.'

'Darcy's going to Verona, to this Arturo guy's sister's wedding.' Darcy had texted her with the mystery man's name and her plans.

'And?'

'He's a guy she met at dance class—the one she went to Rome with.'

He coughed. 'You went to Paris with me.'

She flapped a dismissive hand. 'I've known you for ever, and she barely knows this guy! She says he's a modern-day Indiana Jones.'

'What's the problem?'

She frowned. 'Don't you think it's all a bit…impulsive? Rash?'

'Coming from you, Fizz…'

She brushed the teasing aside. 'Yeah. I know, but I've been like that since I was a toddler. Darcy's not.'

'You said it earlier, maybe Laura's list was to try to make Darcy more like you and you more like Darcy—balance you both out,' Oliver suggested.

'Maybe. Anyway, she was worrying about what to wear, so I sent her a dress. One I bought last year but never got round to wearing.' She sighed. 'At least she'll look and feel fabulous. Just as long as she doesn't end up with a broken heart.'

'Why are you so convinced that she'll end up with a broken heart?'

'I was there when Damian dumped her at the altar. I saw what it did to her,' Fizz said.

'That was a long time ago. She's older and wiser now.' He paused. 'Is that why you hardly ever date? Because you're worried it'll turn out like that for you, too?'

'Mm,' Fizz said. It wasn't a complete fib, but it was only a partial answer.

A full answer was the thing that scared her most. The thing she'd never shared with anyone. She already judged herself and found herself wanting. But if Oli, whose opinion mattered to her, despised her if she told him the truth…

'Fizz, your parents have been married for ever. So have mine. Yes, there are more breakups nowadays than there were thirty years ago, but it doesn't mean that your relationship won't stay the course. How are you ever going to find the right person for you if you never give anyone a chance?'

That was just it. She was beginning to think that maybe Oliver was the right one for her. But would her past—the bits she'd kept from him—mean that she was the wrong one for him?

'You know,' he said, 'when I kissed you by the wisteria, it felt like you kissed me back.'

Panic flooded through her. She didn't want to discuss this. 'We were acting for your parents,' she said. Which was true... up to a point. But even thinking about it made her feel as if all the air had been sucked out of the room. Why was he bringing it up *now*?

She mumbled something else anodyne to brush it off and changed the subject.

But as the days went by, the thought wouldn't go away. It was like having a leaky tap in the kitchen and hearing every drip more loudly than the last. *Tell. Him. The. Truth.*

The longer she left it, the more insistent the voice in her head became. Like a waterfall instead of a drip.

And time was running out to fulfil Laura's bucket list.

Task three: *Do something that scares you.*

If she didn't face her demons and tell Oliver the truth, she wouldn't be able to move forward.

In the end, she messaged him.

Can we talk? Somewhere private, just you and me?

Sure. I'll meet you outside Goodge Street Tube station. I know somewhere nearby. Text me when you're at Camden station.

She was grateful that he didn't ask questions.

She made a fuss of Tilly. 'I won't be long,' she promised. 'I just need to talk to Oli. Tell him the truth.'

She texted him from the platform to let him know that her train was due in two minutes. As he'd promised, he was waiting for her outside Goodge Street station.

'Are you OK?' he asked.

'I'm not sure,' she admitted.

'Let's walk,' he said.

She was glad that he didn't take her arm. She needed to be strong for this. Self-contained.

He led her through a couple of back streets and then into what looked like a Victorian building from the outside but a modern open-plan office inside. He went over to the receptionist, who gave him a key, and he beckoned Fizz to follow him round the corner.

He opened the door onto a tiny courtyard. In the centre was a small knot garden made from box hedges and stuffed with lavender and herbs, and placed casually round the knot garden were several wrought-iron benches. There were a couple of wrought-iron frames, too, with roses planted in their centre; no doubt by the middle of the summer the roses would have climbed all over the frames and be scenting the air.

'This is an amazing space,' she said. 'How did you find out about it?'

'Do you remember my friend Sanjay from uni?' he asked. 'He's a senior account exec at the ad agency here. The agency's a big believer in holistic spaces, and they set up this courtyard a couple of years ago. I asked if I could borrow it for an hour or so.'

'This is beautiful. Butterflies flitting everywhere, birds singing—you'd never believe you were right in the middle of London.'

'And it's private, like you wanted. Just you

and me,' he said. 'I can ask Sanjay for some coffee, if you want.'

She shook her head. 'It's fine. I don't need coffee. I just…' She blew out a breath. 'I don't know where to start, Oli.'

'The beginning's good,' he said. 'Or anywhere that feels comfortable.'

Nothing would feel comfortable about this. 'The third task in my bucket list. Do something that scares me.'

He looked at her, his blue eyes kind. 'That's losing your other sister, isn't it? I know things aren't quite the way you want them to be with you and Darcy at the moment, but I'm sure you can talk it over and work something out.'

'It's not that—though you're right, I do worry about that.' She took a deep breath. Right now, it felt as if she were about to leap off a precipice and she wasn't sure the bungee rope was properly attached. 'I'm going to take a risk. Tell you something I've never told anyone else.'

Oliver had a bad feeling about this. He could see the seriousness in Fizz's expression. Whatever she was going to tell him had clearly hurt her badly. And he didn't have a clue what it was.

She was his best friend, as well as the woman

he'd fallen in love with. He'd known her for years. Why didn't he have the remotest clue what was wrong?

'OK,' he said. 'Just so it's clear, I'll treat whatever you tell me as completely confidential.'

'I already know that. I didn't need to ask.'

It warmed him to know that she trusted him that much. 'Sorry for interrupting. I'm listening,' he said gently.

'It happened just after Laura died.'

Five years ago. He'd been in New York at the time, on business for his father. He'd known that Laura was fading, but he'd hoped he'd be finished in New York and back to support Fizz before Laura actually died.

'A couple of days afterwards, I came back to London to see my tutors and sort out my work. I had a project I knew I needed to work on—something that counted towards my degree, so I couldn't just ignore it—but I didn't want to leave Mum and Dad unsupported before the funeral. They were barely able to put one foot in front of another.'

Understandable. Having to bury your child was any parent's worst nightmare.

'Darcy agreed to stay in Bath for a couple of days, while I sorted out things in London and rearranged my deadline, and then she was going to go back to Edinburgh for a few days and come back for the funeral,' Fizz continued.

Which all sounded fair enough, to him. What was he missing?

'One of my tutors couldn't see me until the day after I got back to London. My house-mates weren't around and my head really wasn't in a good place,' she said. 'I went out that night. I intended to get very, *very* drunk, dance my feet off, and maybe snog someone to make myself feel better.' She closed her eyes. 'Except, the next morning, I woke up in this guy's flat. A place I didn't recognise.'

Now he was starting to understand what the problem was.

'I don't actually remember anything between snogging him on the dance floor and waking up the next morning.' She shook her head. 'I didn't even know his name.'

Fizz clearly felt guilty about having a one-night stand. But that wasn't fair. These things happened. He took her hand. 'Fizz, right then you needed comfort—and sometimes only physical comfort will do. You were free to choose someone to do that for you.' Or was that what he was missing? 'Unless he hurt you or pressured you into it?'

'I don't *think* so. I did wonder if he'd slipped something into my drink, because I couldn't remember very much the next day. Or maybe I'd just drunk more than I thought I had.' She bit her lip. 'Or maybe I just blocked everything out of my head, because I was so ashamed of what I did.'

'Fizz, you have absolutely nothing to be ashamed of. This isn't the Victorian era. You were twenty years old and you were single. If you wanted to sleep with someone, that was your choice and it's nobody else's business.'

Her eyes narrowed. 'You don't think any differently about me?'

'No.' He stroked her hair. 'Of course I don't. Darcy and your parents wouldn't, either. Or any of your friends. I'm sorry you never told me about this before. I could've maybe reassured you that it's nothing to feel bad about. A one-night stand isn't a big deal.' Or was there more to it than that, something that was so subtle it'd gone over his head? He folded his fingers round hers. 'I wish I'd been there, that night, instead of in New York. I knew how ill Laura was and there wasn't much time.

I'm sorry. I should've stayed in London to be there for you.'

'Your dad wanted you to go. It was your first time of doing something for the gallery on your own. You needed to go,' she said. 'And I'm not sure you could've rescued me from what happened.'

'If you'd been with me, nobody would've spiked your drink or anything else,' he said.

She dragged in a breath. 'Thank you. But I could've said no.'

'If you don't remember what happened, then you weren't in a position to say no— or to give consent,' he said. 'Any decent guy would've either made sure you got home to your own place safely and had someone to look after you, or taken you back to his place and kept an eye on you himself, sleeping on the floor instead of taking advantage of you. This isn't on you, Fizz. Please don't beat yourself up about something that wasn't your fault.'

Oh, but the next bit was definitely her fault. She should've predicted it. Done something about it. At least gone to the pharmacy and asked for help, the morning after, instead of blocking it out and refusing to deal with it.

He kept looking at her, his eyes kind, and that gave her the courage to say more.

'That's just the beginning,' she said. 'I guess I wasn't thinking straight. I went back to my place without waking the guy from the night before, because I didn't want to be late for the meeting with my tutor. I showered and changed, then had my meeting. And then I packed everything I needed and I took the train back to Bath. I put everything out of my head. Pretended it hadn't happened.'

Oliver had made it clear he didn't despise her for the one-night stand. But the next bit... How could he not despise her? She closed her eyes again. 'Two weeks later, I realised my period was late. I convinced myself it was because I was upset about Laura.'

He rubbed the pad of his thumb against the back of her hand, still keeping his fingers wrapped round hers. 'It could've been,' he said. 'You were grieving. Stressed.'

'True, but I knew deep down it wasn't that. I felt different,' she said. 'It took me another three days to work up the courage to do a pregnancy test.' She dragged in a breath. 'I went to the supermarket furthest away from home, and just hoped I wouldn't bump into anyone I'd been to school with or who knew my parents. Anyone who might see what I was buying and start gossiping. I put a magazine over the top of the test in my basket to hide it while I was in the shop, and I went through a self-checkout so I wouldn't have to have the test on show for more than a couple of seconds before I stuffed it in my bag. And then I went to the supermarket's toilets and I did the test. I just stared and stared at the test stick in the cubicle, wanting that first line to come up so I knew it was working. And then it seemed to take for ever for the test results to show. I'd just about convinced myself that I was panicking over nothing, and feeling a bit different was just psychological. Obviously it was negative and I had nothing to worry about. I looked away.' She swallowed hard. 'And then I looked back again and the second line was there, out of nowhere. Really dark. There was no chance I could be mistaken. I was definitely pregnant.'

He said nothing, so she risked a glance at him. He looked concerned, but not as if she'd shocked him. 'You're quiet,' she said, a slight edge to her voice.

'I'm listening,' he said, and squeezed her hand briefly. 'Not judging.'

'Thank you,' she said raspily. Her throat

felt constricted, as if something was blocking it. The words she didn't want to say. The words that scared her. The words that needed to come out.

'Keep talking,' he said gently, when she still said nothing. 'It's not going any further than me. Keeping it locked inside you is hurting you. Telling me might make it lose its power.'

His faith in her was enough to make her push on. 'I didn't know what to do, Oli. I wandered round in a bit of a daze. God knows how I managed to find the right bus home. I was in the middle of my degree, I'd just lost my sister, and my life was in enough of a mess as it was. The idea of bringing an unplanned baby into the middle of all that—especially as I didn't even remember the guy's name and I had no way of getting in touch with him...'

'It must've been terrifying,' he said. 'And there was nobody you could talk to? Darcy?'

'She was hurting as much as I was. So were Mum and Dad. I couldn't dump my worries on them.'

'You could have talked to me,' he said. 'I wouldn't have judged you.'

'I felt too guilty. The mess was all of my

own making. If I hadn't gone out that night, or if I'd kept an eye on what I was drinking and not gone home with that guy, or if I'd seen a pharmacist the next day and got the morning after pill—any one of those things would've meant I hadn't screwed up completely.'

'I'm sorry I wasn't there for you,' he said. 'If I'd had any idea, I would've done my best to support you. I hope you know I'll always listen.'

'I'm sorry I shut you out, back then,' she said. 'I think I shut everyone out. I had a bit of a meltdown at home. Everyone thought it was because of Laura's death, and it was easier to let them believe that than to tell the truth. And then…two weeks later, I was on the train, on my way back to London, when I started getting cramps. I went to the loo and realised I was bleeding. I didn't have any sanitary protection with me, and there was no way of buying anything on the train. The only people in my carriage were men, and a couple of women who looked as if they were older than my mum and probably didn't need to carry anything with them any more—nobody I could ask for emergency help. I just had to make do with stuffing toilet roll in my knickers and hoping I wasn't going to leak everywhere. I think that was the worst train journey of my life.'

'Oh, Fizz. That must've been so hard to deal with.'

'I made it to Paddington, and I went straight to the shops so I had something a bit better to help me get back to my flat. And then I stood in the shower and cried until the water went cold.'

Then he moved, scooping her onto his lap. 'If this is the wrong thing, tell me and I'll back off,' he said. 'But right now I'm guessing you could do with a hug.'

'I could.' She squeezed her eyelids shut, willing the tears to stay back, but one slid out anyway. 'Sorry. I'm messing up your shirt.'

'I don't care.' He kept his arms round her. 'It's not important.'

'I feel so guilty.' She could hear the shudder in her own voice. 'I'd messed everything up. And then I lost the baby—I should've been relieved, because it solved my problems, but I felt even worse. I was sure it was my fault because the baby knew it wasn't wanted.'

His arms were warm and comforting round her. 'It wasn't your fault. A lot of babies don't make it through the first three months of pregnancy, and there are all sorts of reasons why. It really *wasn't* your fault,' he repeated. 'You'd already lost Laura; even though the baby wasn't planned, losing it must've been hard.'

She nodded. 'I tried to tell myself I was lucky, because it meant I didn't have to make any difficult choices or even face up to what I'd done. But I was just miserable. I still am, deep down. I couldn't tell Mum, Dad or Darcy, because they were already in bits and they didn't need me dumping an extra load on top of them.'

'What about your personal tutor?'

'He wasn't the most sympathetic of people,' she said. 'And I didn't want any of the tutors I liked thinking as badly of me as I thought of myself.'

He held her a little bit more tightly. 'Any tutor worth their salt would've given you a hug, made you a cup of tea, fed you cake and made you talk. What about one of your housemates?'

She leaned against him. 'It was easier just to let everyone think I was upset because of Laura. And that felt wrong, too—my sister deserved better than that from me. I shouldn't have used her as an excuse to cover up what I did.'

'Laura,' he said, 'would've understood. And I can say that because I met her.'

'I buried myself in work, a bit.' She lifted her head and gave him a wry smile. 'You were good about that. Even though you were busy at the gallery, you always made me feel you had time for me. And you took me to the sea for long walks.'

'I knew you were upset, and I thought it was because of Laura,' he said. 'I worried that you were working too hard because that was the best way to block out your feelings.'

'It was,' she said. 'It helped me cope. Work, and you.'

'When I feel low, walking by water always helps me. Being a bloke, I'm not great at talking about emotional stuff—so I tried to do for you what I knew would help me, and hoped it helped you as well.'

'It did.' She bit her lip. 'I've buried it, Oli. To the point where I can't tell my family now because they'll be hurt that I didn't confide in them years ago. And I'm stuck. Until I've dealt with how it makes me feel, I can't move on.'

'I get that,' he said.

'This is what scares me,' she said softly.

'Talking about it. What I did. The consequences.'

He stroked her hair. 'Everyone makes mistakes, or looks back and wishes they'd done something differently. You were only twenty. You'd handle things differently now because you're older and you've had more life experience. If one of your friends came to you and told you a similar story, you'd support her rather than judging her harshly, wouldn't you?'

'Yes,' she admitted.

'So be kinder to yourself.' He paused. 'Fizz, did you get any kind of medical advice at the time?'

She nodded. 'I went to the student health centre. They did some tests. Whoever he was, he'd taken proper care of his physical health, and I'm beyond grateful for that.'

'That's not what I meant, but I'm glad you didn't have that worry on top of everything else.' He stroked her hair. 'I meant, did they talk to you about why you lost the baby, and how you might feel in the future?'

'Not really,' she said.

'Then maybe it would help you to talk to someone about it.'

'Like who?' she asked.

'A counsellor, a helpline, or someone in a support group—someone who can help you work it through and teach you the tools to deal with how you feel. Obviously you can always tell me anything, and I'll always listen,' he said. 'But I don't know how to make you feel differently about what happened to you. You need to talk to someone professional, someone who knows how to do that.'

'So you don't despise me?'

'Of course I don't despise you. You make my world a much better place. Nothing's going to change that. And, just so you know, that'll be the same for anyone else who knows you.'

'I just felt so ashamed. And guilty. I still do.'

'I think that a lot of people in your shoes would feel like that, even though you've done nothing wrong.' He stroked held her close. 'What do you need, Fizz?'

'I don't know,' she said.

'I want to support you,' he said. 'Right now, I'm terrified that I'm going to say the wrong thing and hurt you. But it's what *you* need that's important right now. So help me out here, a little?'

She blew out a breath. 'I just wanted to be honest with you.'

'I get that,' he said. 'I wish you'd told me before, because I would've been there for you. I hate to think of you carrying all that pain on your own. If you want me to go with you for moral support and wait outside when you do see someone, I'll be there.'

'I think,' she said, 'you're right. That's what I need to do. It scares the hell out of me, opening up like that to a complete stranger…but I need to do it.'

'Whatever you need, tell me and it's yours,' he said. 'If you want me to help you find a counsellor, or just sit in your flat and play with Tilly and keep you company while you're looking, I'm in. No judgements, no telling you what to do.'

'Thank you,' she said. 'For listening. For understanding.'

'Any time,' he said.

And she knew he meant it. Regardless of what happened in their relationship, Oliver Harrison would always be her friend.

But did she want him to be so much more…?

CHAPTER EIGHT

A FEW DAYS LATER, Fizz went to her first counselling session. Oliver accompanied her for
moral support, and while she was in her session he sat in the waiting room reading a
magazine on his phone. When she came out,
her eyes were red, but she looked lighter of
spirit than he'd seen her in a while.

'How did you get on?' he asked.

'It helped.' She gave him a slightly wobbly
smile. 'I've got a way to go, but I'm heading
in the right direction. And thank you for your
support. I'm not sure I would've had the courage to come on my own.'

'Yes, you would,' he corrected. 'And I got
some much-needed reading time, so I have a
lot of nerdy stuff to regale you with. Did you
know that the pattern on top of custard cream
biscuits is meant to be ferns—because of the
Victorian pteridomania?'

Just as he'd hoped, she laughed and tucked

her hand through his arm. 'Oh, Oli. You're *such* a nerd. What's pteridomania? If *ptero* is flying and mania's a craze, then maybe something to do with ballooning?'

'Not even close. It's fern fever,' he said. 'Pteridophytes—ferns—hadn't been studied as much as flowers, so amateur botanists had more of a chance of finding something new.' He grinned. 'They were really popular in decorative arts. You could always add them as a range of jewellery and start the craze going again.'

She shook her head, but she was smiling. 'Where do you get this stuff?'

'It was yet another article in a magazine,' he said. 'My guilty pleasure.'

'Custard creams and fern patterns.' She smiled. 'I think that's our cue to go for a cup of tea and—well, you can have a custard cream, if you like, but I'm thinking warm scones. And it's my shout, because you've been a star.' She hugged into him feeling more content than she ever had before.

The next day, things went in completely the opposite direction. Oliver was just about to leave the gallery for his flat when his mum texted.

Can you call in to see us tonight?

She hadn't mentioned why. His first thought was that his father was ill and she was downplaying it.

He rang her back rather than texting. 'Mum? Is Dad all right?'

'Yes.' But she sounded subdued. Upset, even.

'What's happened?' he asked.

'I'd rather talk about it face to face.'

His hot date tonight was only with some paperwork, and it didn't matter if he got to it later than he'd planned. 'I'm on my way,' he said.

Given that it was rush hour, the Tube was more of a squash than usual, but it was still quicker than driving. He didn't pause to pick up flowers for his mum or a magazine for his dad, the way he usually would; the tone of her voice had alerted him that it'd be better to go straight there.

Juliet Harrison wasn't the needy sort who made a fuss over nothing. If his dad hadn't taken a turn for the worse, what could have upset her?

He rang the doorbell to signal his arrival, then used his key; Poppy the Westie came scampering through to the hallway to welcome him, wagging her tail madly. Oliver stooped to make a fuss of her, then went in search of his parents.

He found his mother in the living room on the sofa. 'Hi, Mum.' He frowned. 'Where's Dad?'

'Having a lie-down.'

That raised a red flag. His father hated resting. Oliver caught his breath. 'Is he having symptoms again?'

'No.'

'Then what's wrong?'

'I had a text from my friend Tamsin this afternoon.' His mother's voice was toneless. 'She sent me a story she thought I'd like. She said it was really romantic and sweet. Which, I suppose, it was.'

'OK.' He was still none the wiser.

Juliet handed her phone to him with the message open. He duly clicked on the link and read the news story.

The article was about a couple who'd recently got engaged in front of Van Gogh's *Sunflowers* in the National Gallery. The bride-to-be's love of sunflowers had inspired what she wanted for an engagement ring—and a brilliant up-and-coming jeweller had designed and made it for them.

Oliver winced as he saw the close-up photograph.

Fizz's borrowed engagement ring.

The ring she'd designed for someone else.

It looked as if he was going to have to come clean about their fake engagement a bit sooner than he'd expected.

'Mum. I can explain.'

'Can you?' Her eyes narrowed. 'You lied to us, Oliver. The pair of you.'

'We didn't mean to hurt anyone,' he said.

'But Fizz made that ring for someone else,' Juliet said quietly. 'And you let us believe it was an engagement ring from you. And we've seen her wearing it since this article came out. What did she do—borrow it from that poor girl every time she saw us?'

'No. She made a replica,' Oliver said. He sighed. 'Mum, will you let me explain?'

She frowned. 'I'm so disappointed in you, Oliver. You lied to us.'

'It wasn't meant to hurt you.' He blew out a breath. 'Mum, you know Dad wants me to settle down and get married before he's happy for me to take over the gallery fully. At my age, you were already married.'

Juliet nodded. 'He just wants to see you settled. We both do.'

'And I will settle down. When I'm ready,' he said. 'When you called me to say Dad had collapsed, I called Fizz. She came straight to the hospital from work—and she was worried enough about you both that she didn't even think about the ring. She'd put it on to check for any last-minute tweaks. Dad saw it, and you both assumed I'd given it to her as an engagement ring.'

'But you didn't correct us. You let us believe it. Both of you.'

'Because,' he said quietly, 'I asked her to. I didn't know if Dad was going to make it or not. In case he didn't pull through that operation, I wanted him to be happy before he went under the anaesthetic. And the idea of us getting married distracted you from worrying quite so much about Dad. That was a good thing.'

She shook her head. 'I'm not a child, needing to be humoured. Neither's your dad. You could have told us the truth at any time since the operation.'

'We were going to tell you,' he said. 'Soon. When Dad was stronger and you were less stressed.'

She ignored the comment. 'Everything you said about your relationship was a lie. She said she loved you.'

Oliver winced. 'I'm her best friend. Of course she loves me.'

'You *behaved* like an engaged couple,' Juliet continued. 'You were kissing by the wisteria— or was that all an act, too?'

He'd meant the kiss. He had a feeling that Fizz might have meant it, too; but when he'd tackled her about it, she'd brushed it aside. Then she'd told him the secrets she'd buried, and he'd dropped the subject because he didn't want to put any pressure on her until she was ready to move forward. And he wasn't going to break his promise about keeping what she'd told him confidential. 'I'm sorry we upset you,' Oliver said. 'Look, let me call Fizz. I'll do it on speaker so you can hear everything I say to her and everything she says to me.'

'I don't think there's any point. Right now, I don't want to talk to her. I'm too hurt and angry,' Juliet said. 'And as for wanting your father to be happy—did you not think about how he'd react when you told him the truth?'

'No,' he admitted. 'I panicked, and I focused on the moment.'

'That's what he said,' Juliet said. 'So how can he trust you with the business? What if something happens and you panic at work? Are you going to tell a pack of lies, get found out, and ruin the gallery's reputation?'

Oliver stared at his mother, horrified. 'Is that what he really thinks I'd do?'

'To the point where he's planning to go back to the office next week.'

'He *can't*. He's supposed to be resting,' Oliver said.

'How can he rest, when he's worrying what you might be doing to the gallery? At least if he's in the office, he can see what's going on and he won't be so worried.'

'I'm running it exactly the same way he would. With integrity,' Oliver said. 'I know you're both hurt and angry, and you have every right to be, but think about it logically, Mum. If anyone at the gallery was concerned about my performance over the last few weeks, they would've had a quiet word with Dad about it long before now.'

'Try convincing your father of that,' Juliet said. 'The way he sees it, if you can lie about being engaged, what else could you lie about? And I can completely see his point.'

It was stress, Oliver told himself. His mum had been worried sick about his dad; right now she was lashing out at him because he was an easy target. She didn't mean it. He needed to calm things down rather than react, even though he was really hurt they seemed to think so little of him. 'I'm sorry,' he said again. 'Yes, I lied, but it was with the best of intentions.'

'Lying isn't a good basis for any kind of relationship,' Juliet said.

'I know,' he said quietly. 'I did what I thought was the right thing, and I was wrong. I'm sorry I've let you down. I'll go and apologise to Dad, and then I'll talk to Fizz.' He bit his lip. 'If Dad has a setback on his health, because of me, I'll never forgive myself.'

When he knocked gently on his parents' bedroom door, there was no answer. He opened the door quietly and could see that his dad was asleep. Rather than waking him, Oliver retreated to his own room and called Fizz.

'You know your couple in the National Gallery? There was a news article about them. Mum's best friend sent it to her.' He paused. 'There was a close-up of the ring.'

'Oh, no.' She sounded horrified. 'I take it

your parents worked the truth out for themselves?'

'Yes. They're pretty upset,' he said. 'You were right. All I did by not being honest with them was to push the reckoning further down the line.'

'I'll come over and explain it's my fault,' she said immediately.

'It *wasn't* your fault,' he said. 'I was the one who asked you to pretend.'

'The least I can do is take half the blame. I should've told them the truth tactfully, there and then, and I didn't.'

He blew out a breath. 'Fizz, please don't come over. They, um, need some distance.'

'Ah.' There was a pause. 'I understand,' she said.

But he'd heard that note of hurt in her voice. Rejection, from a couple who'd always liked her so much and made her welcome. Now she was *persona non grata*. None of this was fair, because it wasn't her fault. He'd fix it, but it would take time. And in the meantime she was hurting.

And his worst nightmare was coming true.

He'd always known that Fizz had had issues about relationships, that she was leery about settling down. He'd thought it was because of seeing her oldest sister jilted at the altar, until she'd told him about what had happened after Laura's death. Fizz didn't believe in love. Friendship she could deal with, but not love. If she knew how he really felt about her, she'd back away—and he'd lose her completely. It was why he'd held back in the past; and telling her now that she was the love of his life would make her back away even faster.

Right at this moment he needed to put his feelings on hold, so he could sort things out with his dad and the gallery; and then he'd have time to sort things out between the two of them. She'd been his best friend for long enough to understand that he needed a little space, right now... hadn't she?

'Fizz. I'll still be there for you. Of course I will. I'll go with you to your appointments. But right now I need to support my parents. Dad's worrying that I'm going to make as much of a mess of the gallery as I have of my personal life—and I need to take the strain off him before it makes him ill again. I haven't worked out how I'll fix things, yet, but I will. It's not you. It's me.' And how horrible he felt, saying that. As if he were dumping her. Which he wasn't, because they weren't really together at all. Even though he wished they were. This was rapidly becoming a horrible mess. And all because he'd wanted to protect his dad, to keep him happy before that life-saving operation… 'It's me being a bloke and not being able to multi-task,' he said, frantically willing her to understand him the way she always had.

'If there's anything I can do, just let me know,' she said.

'Thanks. I will,' he said, knowing that he had no intention of leaning on her—and knowing that she knew it, too. 'And if you need anything, ring me.'

'Of course,' she said, and he knew that she wouldn't. She'd agreed to give him the space he needed to fix things with his family, but at the same time he was pretty sure that she was already backing away from him. He had a nasty feeling that she'd slide quietly out of his life before he could do anything about it, and he didn't have a clue what to say to stop that happening. If he told her he loved her, she'd panic and he'd ruin things between them for ever. If he didn't tell her, he'd lose her. Whatever he did, he lost.

'Take care,' she said. 'And tell your parents I'm sorry.'

* * *

Fizz knew Oliver was right to ask her for some space. He was under enough strain; he didn't need her to add to it.

Just she hadn't expected it to hurt so much.

She'd always called and messaged Oliver as often as she'd called both her sisters: when she heard a joke she thought he'd enjoy or a piece of music he'd love, or came across a painting he'd adore. With Darcy being so far away, Oliver was her go-to person if she wanted to see a film or a play. He was the one she went with if she was trying a restaurant for the first time. He was the one she guinea-pigged when she found an interesting recipe.

Stepping back from him felt *weird*. As if there was an Oliver-shaped space in her life that wasn't going to be filled again. Which was ridiculous: of course she'd see him again. He was her best friend, for pity's sake.

But she knew it wouldn't be quite the same. There would be a new awkwardness between them, thanks to their ridiculous fake engagement. And as for the way she'd thought their relationship was going, after Paris—that was completely out of the question. Hadn't she learned from her sister's example that love didn't last? Hadn't she learned from that dark space after Laura's death that reaching out for love just spelled disaster? Wishing that things were different was just setting herself up for more heartbreak.

She and Oli weren't together. There wasn't going to be a happy ending. She wasn't even sure that their friendship was going to survive this, and she'd been closer to Oli than to anyone else outside her parents and her sisters. And it broke her heart to think that she'd lost his friendship—as well as the chance to make that friendship something deeper.

How, just how, was she going to fix this?

She didn't have a clue. Especially as the person she wanted to talk to about this was the very person she couldn't talk to, right now.

'I have an apology to sort out,' she said to Tilly, stroking the cat's head.

Flowers and an anodyne message written by somebody else weren't enough. She couldn't deliver anything personally; but she could at least give the florist a personal card to go with the flowers.

She sat down at the kitchen table with art paper that she'd folded in half, and did a pen and ink drawing of Poppy the Westie from memory. While it was drying, she drafted a letter.

Dear Juliet and Mark,
I'm so sorry.
    I understand why you don't want to see me at the moment, but I can't just ignore the hurt I've caused you or pretend nothing's happened.
    I want to apologise for not being honest with you right at the start about the ring. I really didn't mean to hurt you. I also don't want to come between you and Oliver. He loves you very much and you're so important to him. He's a good man.
    I misdirected you with the very best of intentions. I'm sorry I got it so wrong, and I hope that you'll find a way to forgive me.
    With love and very best wishes for Mark's continued recovery,

She stopped and read it. How did she sign it? They'd always called her Fizz. But would the more formal Felicity be more appropriate? It wasn't exactly a great letter. Too many of the sentences started with 'I'. Her primary school teacher would've written a red note in the margin: *Try to vary the beginnings of your sentences, Felicity.*

The problem was, she couldn't vary them. Unless she wrote 'we'—and it wasn't fair to drag Oliver into this. That comment about him being a good man could go; his parents already knew that, plus it sounded like sucking up—even though it wasn't and she really meant it. The rest of her message was heartfelt, and she hoped they'd take it in the spirit with which she'd written it.

She held the card she'd drawn at an angle to the light to check that the ink was dry, then opened it and wrote up her draft in her neatest handwriting. In the end, she signed it 'Fizz'. She found an envelope for it, then made a fuss of Tilly. 'I'll take this to the florists as soon as they open tomorrow.'

In the meantime, she was glad of some routine accounts work to take her mind off things, and then re-runs of a favourite comedy with Tilly curled up in her lap.

The next morning, Fizz called in to her local florists for a chat; they promised to arrange a nice summery bouquet and deliver it to Ju-

liet along with Fizz's card in the early afternoon. Then she headed to Covent Garden to
drop off some more stock at the shop that
sold her flower earrings—including the first
wisteria ones.

She loved the buzz of the market: the
turquoise-painted wrought-iron arches and
glass panes of the roof, the ancient paving
stones in the piazza, the stalls crammed with
arts and crafts, the scent of freshly baked
cookies and coffee, the old-fashioned shop
fronts with their hanging signs outside, the
opera singer in the corner downstairs whose
voice soared above the hubbub of the tourists'
chatter, and the jugglers and poets entertain-
ing everyone with street theatre in between
the market and the Roman temple-like façade
of the church. Just as it had been for hundreds
of years; the first Punch and Judy show in
England had been performed near here, wit-
nessed by Samuel Pepys and recorded in his
diary.

But there were quiet spots in Covent Garden, too: only a few steps from the bustle of
the Apple Market and Jubilee Market were the
gardens behind St Paul's church. The wooden
benches with their brass memorial plaques, in-

terspersed with old-fashioned lamps, lined the alley between the two stretches of garden. The trees were in full leaf and the gardens themselves were full of early summer flowers. At this time of day, in the half-hour before lunchtime, the gardens were almost empty; just the occasional bench was occupied by somebody reading a book.

A quiet space to think about what she wanted...

The last task of her bucket list.

This would fit the bill perfectly.

Fizz walked over to the Diamond Jubilee Memorial on the south side of the church, an oversized cast-iron replica of a penny surrounded by a maze of red and yellow bricks. Walking a maze was meant to be like a meditation, wasn't it? And maybe that would help her think. So she duly walked it.

What did she want?

Before Paris, she would've said that she already had everything she wanted. A family she loved, a job she loved, and good friends.

Laura's bucket list and Paris had changed everything.

She'd gone to Paris with Oliver, and seen him in a different light—as a man, rather than just as her best friend.

She'd made a commitment, and now she had an elderly ginger cat who'd adapted to her routines and just liked being with her.

She'd done something that scared her: she'd finally faced up to what had happened, five years ago. Her badly managed one-night stand. The unplanned pregnancy that had sent her into a spiral of panic—and then the miscarriage that had made her feel so horribly guilty. It would still take a while for her to work it through, but she realised that it was time to stop beating herself up about it. To let herself move on.

So what did she want now?

The more she thought about it, the more she realised.

What she wanted was Oliver. Not just as her best friend, but as her partner. A man who'd always have her back, but who was also strong enough to let himself lean on her when he needed support. A man who loved her family, and they loved him right back. A man whose family loved her, too—well, they *had* loved her, she amended silently. If she could persuade them to accept her apology, maybe they'd find their way back to a warm, easy relationship, in time.

But the question was: did Oliver want her?

His dad wanted him to settle down and get married; but Oliver hadn't asked her to marry him. He hadn't even suggested it as a remote possibility. So all the stuff in Paris: had they both just been carried away by the romantic atmosphere in the City of Love? And those kisses since their fake engagement: had he felt anything at all for her, beyond their friendship?

Plus she'd told him the worst about herself. Things she'd kept secret for years and years. He'd been supportive and kind: but had he started having second thoughts about her? Now he knew what a mess she was beneath the surface, would he quietly back away? Had he used his dad's health as an excuse to put another barrier between them—the whole 'it's not you, it's me' routine?

Walking round a tiny, easy-to-solve maze wasn't the relaxing, meditative experience it was meant to be. Instead, it raised more questions and made her feel even more mixed-up. Miserable. Wishing things were different and not knowing how to change them.

She needed to talk this through with someone. Oliver would be her go-to whenever she wanted to tease out a knotty problem; but she could hardly talk to him about himself, could she?

She texted Darcy.

Are you free to talk some time today? Could do with some advice xx

The reply was almost immediate.

In wall-to-wall meetings. Will ring you tonight xx

In the meantime, maybe she ought to do the same: go back to her flat, make a fuss of Tilly, and get on with her work. Suppressing the ache in her heart, and hating the fact that she missed Oli so much—how, how, *how* hadn't she realised before what she really felt about him?—she texted back,

Thanks xx

Later that evening, Darcy video-called her. 'Are you all right, Fizz?'

'Yes.' She sighed. What was the point in pretending? She'd wanted to talk to her sister about this. 'No, actually, I'm not. I've made a huge mess of things.'

'How?'

'I don't even know where to start.' She blew out a breath. 'I think the only thing I did right was the commitment bit—I've got Tilly, and she's settled in really well.' She angled the camera so Darcy could see the ginger cat snoozing happily on Fizz's lap, her paws tucked neatly under her.

'Good. So has Ruby. And I'm enjoying the walks.'

'Good. And the wedding in Verona went all right?'

'Yes. Thank you for the dress. It wasn't what I'd have picked for me, but you were right. I felt amazing in it.'

'That's brilliant.'

'Tell me what's wrong, Fizz,' Darcy said softly. 'I can see it in your face.'

'Oliver,' Fizz said. 'When we went to Paris, I thought I was being clever in booking an Airbnb, and getting a good deal that meant we could stay for two nights instead of one.'

'A wild twenty-four hours and then a bit more. I'd have done that, too,' Darcy agreed. 'What happened?'

'It was tiny. I had no idea that a "studio" would mean a double bed that took up most of the space, a bistro table and two chairs, and a microwave.'

Darcy laughed. 'It isn't as if you were going to cook anything. Not with all those bistros around.'

'No, but I did expect the apartment to have a sofa as well as a bed.'

'So you slept with Oli?'

'Sleeping only as in snoozing, not sex. But I could've done. And waking up in his arms… I started seeing him in a different way, Darcy. And we danced together by the Seine. Drank cocktails—well, I did, after that first disgusting mouthful of absinthe. He stuck to wine.'

'I could've told you that absinthe tastes pants.' Darcy laughed. 'You only ever do it once.'

'Never again,' Fizz agreed. And it felt so good to laugh with her sister. As if the distance she'd felt between them had snapped short again.

'OK. So you thought about having sex with your best friend.'

'I didn't actually have sex with him,' Fizz said. 'But then it got complicated. His dad's been having heart trouble, and he collapsed. Oli rang me, so of course I went to support them.' She sucked in a breath. 'I'd been working on an engagement ring. I was just doing the final "squint and see if anything needs fixing" bit when Oli rang. I could hear how upset he was, so I just dropped everything to go to the hospital, and I kind of forgot I was wearing the ring. And his parents...they thought Oli and I had sneaked off to Paris to get engaged. They were so happy.'

'But that's good, isn't it?'

'No. Because we lied to them,' Fizz said. 'We were going to tell them the truth when Mark was feeling better. But I liked being engaged. I liked doing all the family stuff, and walking hand in hand, and stealing kisses. No, I more than liked it—I *loved* it, Darcy. It's what I never realised I always wanted.'

'Oli's always been in love with you, Fizz so what's the problem?'

'Oli isn't in love with me,' Fizz corrected. Because he wasn't, was he? Or he would've asked her to marry him when his dad had first given him the ultimatum. Or at any time since. Or at least told her how he felt about her—and he hadn't. 'And my client's story was in an online magazine about getting engaged in front of the *Sunflowers* in the National Gallery. The magazine featured a picture of the ring, and Juliet saw it. And Oli's parents are really upset with us.'

'They'll get over it. It's not as if you did it to cheat them out of anything. You just didn't want to tell them the truth while they were already so worried over Mark's heart,' Darcy said. 'Or is there more to this than what you're telling me?'

Caught by sisterly intuition. But she'd promised herself that she'd tell Darcy. 'There's something more,' Fizz said. 'Like I said, I finished the bucket list. I did something that scared me. I told Oli something I've never told anyone else. And I want to tell you in advance that I'm sorry I kept you out of the loop.' She clenched her fists for a moment, and then told Darcy about the one-night stand, the pregnancy and the miscarriage.

'Oh, Fizz. I'm so sorry you went through all that—and even sorrier that you went through it on your own. Why didn't you tell me, honey?'

'Because you, Mum and Dad were already in bits,' Fizz said, feeling miserable. 'You didn't need me making things worse.'

'You're my little sister. You can *always* tell me anything,' Darcy said fiercely, 'no matter what else is going on in my life. Oh, honey. I'm so sorry.'

'I'm telling you now,' Fizz said. 'And I'm OK. Really, I am. Because Oli talked me into going for counselling, and it's helping.'

'Good.'

'The counsellor said I needed to talk to you about it. To Mum and Dad.'

'It's your place to tell them, not mine. But I'll be there when you tell them, if you want me to support you,' Darcy said. 'And I'm proud of you. What you did is a *lot* scarier than going to ballroom dancing lessons.'

'You would've been brave enough to tell us, in my shoes,' Fizz said.

'And you wouldn't be scared by something as pathetic as ballroom dancing,' Darcy said. 'You'd just throw yourself in and have fun.'

'I think,' Fizz said, 'Laura gave us those lists to make us balance out. Be more like each other. Me more of a planner, and you more spontaneous.'

'Maybe you're right.' Darcy paused. 'And that means you've done the fourth thing—the thinking about what you want.'

Fizz nodded. 'Today. In the gardens behind St Paul's in Covent Garden.'

'And what do you want, Fizz?' Darcy asked, her voice gentle.

'Oli,' Fizz said simply. 'Except, in the circumstances…' She shook her head. 'He said we needed some space. And I'm scared he's going to back away from me for ever, now he knows what a mess I am. I mean—love doesn't really work, does it?'

'If you mean what Damian did when he dumped me at the altar, he actually did us both a favour. We weren't right together. It would've been a mistake. But love—love really exists, Fizz,' Darcy said urgently. 'And Oli loves you as more than just a friend—I'm sure of it. He asked you for space because of his parents. But if you talk to them, open up to them, they'll see you didn't mean any harm,' Darcy paused. 'You need to talk to Oli. Properly. Tell him how you really feel about him. And, you know, there's nothing in the rulebook that says he has to be the one to propose. There's no reason why you can't make him an engagement ring and ask him.'

Fizz blinked. 'You do know how long it takes to make a properly nice ring?'

'You're one of the Bennett sisters. You can do anything,' Darcy reminded her. 'Improvise. Use a bit of tinfoil and put a sticker on it or something!'

Fizz couldn't help laughing. 'That's silly.'

'But you'll both always remember it. It'll be one of those stories you bring up and smile about, year after year.'

Her sister had a valid point. 'What about you and Arturo?' Fizz asked.

Darcy smiled. 'I'll tell you more when you've talked to Oli and reported back to me. Not a word before that.'

'That's *cheating*.' But Fizz was smiling when she ended the call.

Proposing to Oli.

That would be taking a huge, huge risk. All her doubts came back. What if he said no?

On the other hand, what if he said yes?

She hadn't spoken to or texted him for a day. That barely counted as space. Then again, they talked and texted all the time, so a whole day probably did count as space. It was a lot longer than she was used to.

And, if she was honest with herself, she missed him. Bone-deep missed him. Without him, her life felt flat. Miserable. Full of shadows. 'I'm Felicity Bennett, and I can do anything,' Fizz told Tilly, stroking the sleeping cat. If Oli said no, at least her proposal would make him realise that she didn't see him as a just a friend—and maybe, if he thought about it a bit more, that no might turn to a yes. All she had to do was be brave enough to carry this through. Reach out for what she wanted. Believe that love could really be hers.

She typed a message to Oliver.

Meet me at Shakespeare's Tree, Primrose Hill, in an hour?

It took him a while to answer, but eventually he sent a message back.

OK.

So far, so good, Fizz thought. Now to sort out the ring.

CHAPTER NINE

As she crossed the road and started to walk
up Primrose Hill, Fizz's heart was thudding—
and not from the exertion of walking up the
slope.

Was Darcy right, and Oliver had been in
love with her for years? Or had her sister mistaken deep friendship for something else?

What if he said no?

What if she ruined their friendship? Then
again, their fake engagement might already
have done most of the work for her when it
came to wrecking their friendship.

What if…?

And then she stopped thinking as she saw
Oli. Casually dressed, in jeans and a T-shirt,
sitting under the tree and reading something
on his phone.

'Hey,' she said.

He looked up and gave her a slow smile.
'Hey, yourself.'

What now? Would he kiss her cheek, the way he usually did? Give her a hug? Stay at a distance?

And why on earth did she feel so ridiculously shy around him?

He stood up in one lithe, graceful movement, and slid his phone into his pocket. How had she never noticed until these last few weeks just how gorgeous he was? 'Any particular reason why you wanted to meet under Shakespeare's Tree?' he asked.

'"*Shall I compare thee to a summer's day?*"' she quoted.

'"*Thou art more lovely and more temperate,*"' he quoted back. 'Are we really trying to out-sonnet each other, Fizz?'

'No,' she admitted. 'I just thought this was an easier place to meet, and it might be quieter than the viewpoint at the top.'

'You're right.' He smiled. 'Mum loved your flowers, by the way. She cried when she read your card. And she wants to frame that sketch of Poppy.'

'Good tears or bad tears?'

'Probably a bit of both,' he said. 'She's going to ring you tomorrow. I'm pretty sure she wants to make things up with you.'

Fizz dipped her head in acknowledgement. 'How's your dad doing?'

'OK. Better than yesterday. He's calmed down and being reasonable, and he's stopped saying that he has to go back to the office.' He raised an eyebrow. 'So. You wanted to talk?'

'I do. I…um…spoke to Darcy this evening. I told her about what happened when I came back to London. And the baby.'

'Good,' he said. 'How did she take it?'

'Pretty much the same as you did,' Fizz admitted. 'And I've done the fourth thing on Laura's bucket list.'

'Did you go to the beach?'

'No. To the garden behind St Paul's in Covent Garden. It's a good space.'

'Uh-huh.'

'I did a lot of thinking,' she said. 'About you, mainly.'

'Should I be worried?'

'I don't know,' she admitted. And it was crazy. She knew him so well, her best friend of years and years and years—but she didn't have a clue how he was going to react to this. Whether the world was going to feel full of sunshine afterwards or full of freezing rain. 'Darcy says you've been in love with me for years.'

'Does she, now?' he asked coolly.

What did that mean? That Darcy was wrong? Or that she was right? He hadn't admitted it. He hadn't denied it. He hadn't asked why she wanted to know.

All her ability to assess a situation seemed to have deserted her.

And since when had Oliver had a perfect poker face? Since when had she been unable to read his mood? It worried her even more, but she needed to ask.

'Is she right?'

'Why?' he riposted.

She narrowed her eyes at him. 'It's rude to answer a question with a question.'

'It's rude to ask someone if they've been in love with you for years,' he shot back.

She raked a hand through her hair, wishing she'd tied it back. Stupid to think that he might be swayed by a pretty dress and canvas shoes; Oliver was a lot deeper than that. And all this verbal sparring with him, much as she normally enjoyed it, really wasn't helping her nerves. This was too important to get wrong.

Maybe she should try another way. Being honest.

'I followed Laura's instructions. I found a quiet place to think, and I walked the Jubilee

Memorial. You know, the little brick maze with the huge penny in the middle.'

'Using the maze as a meditation rather than a puzzle?' he asked.

She nodded. 'And I thought about what I really wanted. I've already got most of it: a family I love, a job I love, a flat I love. A cat.' She sucked in a breath. 'It might be considered greedy to want something more.'

'It might,' he agreed.

'But I do. I want more. I want…' Her throat dried.

'What do you want, Fizz?' he asked softly.

'I want a partner. Someone who'll always have my back but will let me take care of him when he needs it. Someone who doesn't mind that I'm a scatty daydreamer, and will even dream with me if I ask. Someone who brings out my nerd tendencies. Someone I can laugh with and feel safe enough to cry with.'

'And do you have anyone in mind?' he asked.

'I do,' she said. 'I think I've always known, deep down. Except I didn't think he thought of me in that way. I assumed he saw me as a kind of little sister. We kissed, once, but he was the one who called a halt, so I thought I'd got it wrong.'

He was very still, and his eyes were very, very blue. Like a fathomless ocean.

'After that, I think subconsciously I measured everyone I dated against him. They weren't even close, so they never lasted more than three dates. Everyone thought I was being a flaky party girl, but I wasn't,' she said. 'I just didn't connect it up properly. I didn't realise what was right in front of my eyes. That everything I wanted was in reach and I didn't have to go looking and discarding.'

'Go on.' There was a slight raspiness to his voice that told her this was important to him, too. That he felt it as intensely as she did. It gave her the courage to go on.

'He kissed me again,' she said, 'and then I knew. I knew he was the one I'd been looking for all along. The one who makes me feel complete.'

When he didn't say anything, it gave her hope. He wasn't pushing her away. She could do this. Follow through with her plan.

She dropped to one knee, fumbled in her bag, and brought out a small plastic box. 'Oliver Harrison, will you marry me?'

He blinked. 'You're offering me a ring?'

This was where he'd either laugh, or he'd

reject her. And she really, really wasn't sure which it would be. 'Yes,' she said.

'An engagement ring,' he checked.

'A *temporary* engagement ring.' She had to be honest.

'Temporary?' He removed the lid to reveal the neatly made tinfoil ring with its heart-shaped honeycomb 'gem'.

'Ah. I think I understand "temporary",' he remarked.

'Limited shelf life,' she said, spreading her hands. Was that amusement in his eyes? Or horror?

'Representing a yellow gem,' he said. 'Now, what would that be?'

This was Oli. She was pretty sure he was expecting her to give him the nerdy answer. 'It could be amber, or a citrine, or a topaz, if you're looking at a budget option. Tourmaline. Danburite.'

The corner of his mouth quirked. *'Danburite?* Is that something you just made up?'

She shook her head. 'It's a silicate, similar to topaz.'

'I see.'

'At the top end of gems, it could be a yellow sapphire or a fancy yellow diamond. Heat-treated, lab-grown or natural.'

He nodded and gestured to the ring. 'And this is?'

'Honeycomb,' she admitted. 'I cut it myself. With a kitchen knife, not my jeweller's saw.'

'I should hope so. And you attached it to the tinfoil with…?'

'Melted chocolate. And I hope it hasn't melted again, or it'll fall off the tinfoil before you can put it on.'

He grinned, peeled the honeycomb off the tinfoil, and ate it.

'Oli! You were supposed to treat that with reverence, not eat it!' she said indignantly. 'Look at me, Oliver Harrison. I'm down on one knee, asking you to marry me. And what do you do? Instead of answering, you eat the engagement ring I just made for you.'

'Just the gem,' he said. 'The ring's still here.' He dangled the tinfoil off his little finger.

'How can I get engaged to you with a bit of crumpled tinfoil?' she asked.

'Don't forget the honeycomb. Which, I admit, was quite inventive,' he said. He took her hand and drew her to her feet.

'You didn't answer my question,' she said. 'So I take it that was a no to my proposal.' Except he hadn't let go of her hand. She had no idea what was going on in his head.

'I asked you to tell me what you wanted, Fizz.' He paused. 'Are you going to ask me what *I* want?'

Hope quickened in her veins. 'What do you want, Oliver?'

'A long time ago,' he said, 'I was a hard-working student, doing a Master's in Arts and Cultural Management. One night, I went to a party. I started talking to a girl, and we ended up talking all night. We watched the sun rise together, here on Primrose Hill. And it felt as if I'd known her for my entire life. She just *fitted*. But she was eighteen and I was twenty-one, and I could hardly tell her that I wanted to marry her right there and then. She still had a world to conquer. But I could be her best friend. So that's what I was.'

Then Darcy was right and Oliver *had* been in love with her for years?

'One day, she told me she'd had the worst news in the world. She was crying. I wanted to wave a magic wand and make everything all right, though I knew that wasn't possible. All I could do was to hold her close. And then she kissed me. It was amazing. Like fireworks going off in my head. I wanted more, but I knew she was vulnerable and I wasn't going to take advantage of that. I wanted her to want me for myself, not for comfort. So I called a halt, and I told myself I needed to stay in the friend zone.'

All that time they'd wasted, Fizz thought. But she didn't interrupt. Oliver still hadn't actually told her what he wanted.

'And then,' he said, 'she took me to Paris. On a budget, to fit in with her sister's bucket list. Which was possibly the worst place in the world I could go with her: how could I keep telling myself that we were just good friends, when there was all that romance around us? How was I going to resist kissing her, or telling her I loved her?'

She looked at him. 'But you *did* resist it. You didn't kiss me, and you didn't tell me you loved me.'

'I didn't kiss you,' he said. 'Because I was scared that, if I did, it'd make you back off. But I told you I loved you. You might've been too tipsy to remember.'

'The night we had cocktails?' She looked at him. 'But I felt it, the night before. When you took me dancing. You swept me off my feet. I didn't have a clue you could dance like that. But you made me feel special, as if I were floating on air. You weren't my best friend any more. You were this incredibly sexy, funny guy who made my heart do a backflip when you smiled. You quoted romantic French poetry at me—and instead of making me tease you, it made me feel all gooey and mushy. And it was thrilling—as well as scaring the hell out of me.'

'It made me feel all over the place, too,' he said. 'But it wasn't just Paris. It was the way, back in England, when the bottom dropped out of my world and you were there. Supporting me. Making things better.' He shook his head. 'That fake engagement stuff—part of me wanted it to be real, right from the start, but I knew you had issues about love, after seeing that guy break your sister's heart at the altar.'

'But I realise now that wasn't love. He was self-centred and utterly wrong for my sister,' she said. 'And I think now I used it as an excuse. I was scared of what love could do when it went wrong, and it was safer not to give it the chance to go right. Except it was right under my nose, all the time. It took me long enough to work it out.' His eyes were deep, deep cornflower blue. Like a midsummer night. It would be so easy to lose herself there. She caught her breath. 'And Laura's bucket list made me face it head-on. Made me work out what I wanted from life.' She swallowed hard. 'You. That's what I want. That's why I asked you to marry me.'

'With a ring made from a piece of honeycomb stuck to tinfoil with chocolate.' His mouth quirked again.

'Which you *ate*,' she reminded him. 'You were supposed to say yes, not seize the chance to stuff your face with sweeties.'

He grinned. 'I think we need to take a rain check and reframe this.'

Fizz stared at him. 'Are you going to be sexist about it and insist on being the one to propose?'

'Sweet as your honeycomb gesture was…'

He paused long enough for her to laugh and say, 'Yes, I saw what you did there.'

He swirled his free hand in acknowledgement. 'I want to be the one doing the flashy proposal stuff. I've waited a lot of years to do it. It's not being sexist. I just really, really want to be the one who says the words. If you'll humour me.'

'Of course.' She waited expectantly, but he didn't drop to one knee.

'Not here,' he said softly. 'Primrose Hill has different memories for me. Of the night I discovered it really was possible to fall in love with someone, the first time you met them.'

'Why didn't you say anything to me before?' she asked.

'Wrong time, wrong place. And I'm not going to say the words yet either,' he said. 'I'm a planner. I have a particular time and place in mind. Oh, and I have a commission for you. I need an engagement ring. That is, unless you'd rather I asked someone else to make it?'

'No way am I letting someone else make my engagement ring,' she said. 'What do you have in mind?'

'Something that sparkles, like the way you make me feel,' he said. 'Unless you don't like sparkly rings?'

'I admit I'm not keen on pavé rings, but I do like a well-cut gem,' she said.

'It's your choice what you make. Just as long as you wear it for me.'

She smiled. 'I already know what I'll design.'

He smiled back. 'A sunflower?'

'No. That's Laura's flower. For me, I was thinking a forget-me-not: a round brilliant-cut yellow diamond in the centre, with five pear-cut sapphires the same colour as your eyes,' she corrected.

'Do forget-me-nots have five petals?' he checked.

'Oh, you pedant.'

'Details specialist,' he corrected.

She laughed. 'Actually, they do. But, even if they didn't, I'd still make an uneven number of petals.'

He tipped his head slightly to one side. 'Why?'

'Think about it. *"He loves me, he loves me not,"*' she said. 'Even is bad. Odd is good.'

'Hmm,' he said. *'"Doubt thou the stars are fire:/ Doubt that the sun doth move;/ Doubt truth to be liar;/ But never doubt I love."'*

'Would it be pedantic to point out that we know the stars aren't fire, now?' she asked.

'And incorrect. Because, when those lines were written, people believed the stars were fire,' he said.

'You're such a nerd, Oli.'

'Takes one to appreciate one,' he said, and leaned forward to kiss her.

It was a long, slow, sweet kiss, full of promise and pent-up longing. The sort of kiss that could break a heart and stick it back together with sunshine. And it made her knees go weak.

'How quickly can you make that ring?' he asked when he broke the kiss.

'I need to source the gems. And I'll need a hallmark on the ring—I can cut down on the time that takes if I take it to the Assay Office myself and get it done priority.'

'Are we talking days, weeks, months?' he checked.

'Days, if I can get hold of the right gems,' she said. 'I'll check in with my usual dealer first thing tomorrow. And you can come with me, if you like.'

'I'd like that.' He nodded. 'Days. All right. So if I book something for Friday, perhaps we can finish this conversation then.'

'This Friday?' she asked, and thought about it. 'It'll be a bit of a squeeze, but I'll rise to the challenge.'

'Of course you will. You're Fizz Bennett. I'll let you know details as soon as I've sorted it,' he said.

From the way he'd suggested it—using the same words she had when booking their wild twenty-four hours in Paris—she was pretty sure that was where he was going to propose. And she had a feeling that he was going to be inventive about it.

In answer, she kissed him. Together, they walked back down the hill, their arms wrapped round each other. Even though the sun was setting and it was starting to get the tiniest bit chilly, the world felt bright and full of sunshine.

They hadn't said the words, but she knew it. She knew it in her heart. Oli loved her, and she loved him. And everything was going to be OK.

'I assume you're coming back to mine?' she asked. 'Much as I love your parents, I don't want to…' Her voice faded with embarrassment.

He nibbled her earlobe. 'You don't want to make love with me for the first time with anyone else in the house?'

Her cheeks flamed. 'Yeah.'

'God, you're pretty when you blush.' He spun her round into his arms. 'You know what? I'm seriously thinking about being old-fashioned.'

'You mean, no sex until we're married? No *way*,' she said.

'Waiting until we're engaged,' he corrected. 'I've waited seven years for you, Fizz. I can wait until Friday.'

Was he teasing her? But then she saw the seriousness in his face. 'Oli.' She pressed her palm lightly against his cheek. 'You've waited seven years for me to come to my senses and realise that you're the love of my life. I've worked it out, now. So why wait any longer?'

'Because I want it to be special,' he said.

'Being spontaneous now doesn't mean that our engagement night won't be special,' she said.

'I want to have the fun of wooing you. An old-fashioned courtship. Concentrated into one evening.' He caught her lower lip briefly between his. 'And then, just you and me. A wide, wide bed.'

She went hot all over. 'All right,' she agreed huskily.

'I'm going to see you home, kiss you chastely at the door—and on Friday...'

The promise and the look in his eyes were delicious.

It was strange, working on your own engagement ring, Fizz thought. Technically, it was the second time, because she'd made the replica ring for her fake engagement; but this felt different.

And she thought of Oliver with every moment she spent crafting the ring.

He still hadn't actually *said* the three little words to her. That declaration from *Hamlet* wasn't quite enough. And even though she knew how he felt, she wanted to hear the actual words so she could be absolutely certain that he, Oliver Harrison, loved her, Felicity Bennett, and wanted to spend the rest of his days with her. Clearly he was going to wait until he asked her to marry him before saying it.

On Friday.

When they'd be in Paris, which was all that he'd told her.

And she had absolutely no idea what he'd planned, because he'd flatly refused to be drawn into giving her any more details.

Would he ask her to marry him by the clock in the Musée d'Orsay, his favourite place in Paris? By the banks of the Seine, where they'd danced together under the stars? Had he booked the tiny studio apartment in St Ouen and he'd put the ring in the mini-fridge under a pastry to tease her? Or maybe he'd ask her to marry him underneath the huge cherry tree in the Jardin des Plantes, with blossom falling like confetti? The café in the Marais where he'd fed her a rainbow of *macarons*—perhaps with the ring hidden in the middle of a pyramid of her favourite flavours? Or somewhere she hadn't even thought of?

Oliver wasn't as predictable as he seemed.

And she liked that, too: it meant he was reliable, but he was also flexible. The perfect combination.

Once satisfied with the ring, she took it for hallmarking; and she gave him a crimson velvet-covered box with the finished product on Thursday evening.

He opened the box and looked at it. 'I loved that sunflower you made—but this is definitely more you,' he said. 'It's beautiful.'

'Thank you.' She smiled at him.

'Ready for tomorrow?' he asked.

'All packed and ready. And I bet I'm at the station before you are,' she said.

She was wrong. He was already there when she walked into St Pancras, waiting for her by the check-in desk. 'I have coffee,' he said. 'And lunch. Which is a lot more civilised than having to be here at six o'clock in the morning.'

'You've already missed the best part of the day,' she said.

He kissed her, then whispered in her ear, 'Tell me that tomorrow morning.'

And she went hot all over as the possibilities bloomed in her head.

He'd booked them on the train, on the grounds that it was better for the environment—but, unlike their first trip to Paris, he'd booked them in business class. He'd bought them a wonderful picnic for lunch with salads, herbed chicken and flatbreads, followed by lemon tart. And at the Gare du Nord in Paris they were met by a car that took them to a very plush hotel that had been renovated from one of the old Parisian mansions, all cream-coloured walls and huge windows and wrought-iron Juliet balconies. Their suite had an enormous bed, the kind of carpet you sank into, and a stunning view of the Eiffel Tower. And the bathroom alone was bigger than the whole apartment they'd shared a few weeks ago.

'So you're going for the opposite of what we had in St Ouen, then?' She tutted. 'What on earth are we going to do without that micro-kitchen?'

'Room service,' he retorted with a grin. 'Right now, we're dropping our bags, and we have a date at the Louvre.'

She was dressed casually, with comfortable shoes for walking and a sunhat; but she'd brought a dress with her at his request, and hung it up in the wardrobe so any creases would fall out while they were exploring the city. She noticed that he, too, hung up a suit and shirt.

Their hotel wasn't far from the Louvre; he'd arranged skip-the-line tickets, and Fizz thoroughly enjoyed wandering round the galleries hand in hand with him. He took her to the Egyptian gallery to see the Sphinx of Tanis and the incredible painted statue of the Seated Scribe; and she loved the jewellery, from the gold bangle made from two intertwined serpents to the incredible detail on the tiny ducks sitting on a ring.

Every corner seemed to bring a new and famous masterpiece: the *Venus de Milo*, Canova's incredibly romantic *Psyche Revived by Cupid's Kiss*, the *Mona Lisa*. Though Vermeer's *The Lacemaker* was the painting that took her breath away. 'It's the light,' she said to Oliver. 'And I can't believe he managed to squeeze all that detail into such a tiny painting.'

He'd booked skip-the-line tickets for the Eiffel Tower, too, and they zoomed up to the very pinnacle in the glass-sided elevator to drink pink champagne and gaze over stunning views of Paris.

Oliver, Paris and art. It didn't get any better than that, she thought.

Except it did. Because the dinner reservation he'd made for them was at their own private terrace at the hotel. There was a table with a white starched tablecloth, and all around it were white pillar candles and arrangements of deep red roses. A cascade of the de Ronsard roses wound round the wrought-iron railings, and a piano piece she recognised as Debussy played softly from a hidden speaker. In front of them was the Eiffel Tower, and the sky was a riot of colour.

Oliver looked incredible in a dark suit, crisp white shirt, and a blue silk tie with tiny forget-me-nots on it. She'd dressed up, too, in a simple sleeveless round-necked navy dress with a flared skirt and an overlay of chiffon embroidered with tiny white flowers, teamed with her favourite red court shoes.

'You look amazing,' he said.

'So do you,' she said.

Because tonight was special.

Not a surprise engagement, but one that had been a long time in the making. Seven years. Seven years when the most patient man in the universe had been by her side, her best friend.

The food was exquisite and beautifully presented. Scallops with sage butter, spiced squash risotto with greens, and then a *café gourmand*: a beautifully bitter espresso served with four tiny desserts.

'This is perfect. I would never have been able to choose between a tarte tatin, a crème brûlée, a passionfruit *macaron* and raspberries with Chantilly cream,' she said in delight.

'I know. This is the best of all worlds,' he said.

When they'd finished and the table had been cleared, he glanced at his watch. 'Right this very second, I feel more nervous than if I was having a *viva*, a driving test and a really important job interview, all at the same time. Oh, not to mention being a client's proxy at an auction when it was their favourite painting in the world and someone was bidding against us and I was getting near the agreed limit.'

'It's four little words, Oli. And you were the one who insisted on saying them,' she reminded him. 'If you'd accepted my beautifully carved honeycomb ring instead of scoffing it…'

He laughed. 'Yeah. But I'm still nervous. Because this is the most important question I'll ever ask in my entire life.' He took a deep breath. 'Fizz. I fell in love with you the day I met you. You're like a ripple of champagne in the sunshine, spreading light and brightness wherever you go. And I love everything about you. I love the way you can't suppress a smile when you're supposed to be serious. I love the way you focus when you're making something delicate out of what looks to everyone else like little lumps of stone and bits of wire—but in your head you've already seen what their potential really is. I love the way you find joy, that you follow your impulses even when they land you in trouble, and that your heart's big enough to take on an elderly cat whose owner died, so she can enjoy her sunset years with you.' He glanced at his watch again. 'I'm running out of time. Felicity Bennett, I love you so much. You really are my best friend. My soulmate. I want to spend the rest of my life with you, make babies with you if we're lucky, and have a house full of love and laughter.' He stood up, walked round the table to her chair, and dropped down on one knee. 'Will you marry me?' He opened the crimson velvet box to display the gorgeous forget-me-not sapphire and diamond engagement ring she'd made.

She leaned forward to kiss him. 'I love you, too, Oliver Harrison. Yes, I'll marry you.'

There was a perfectly timed burst of sparkling in front of them as the Eiffel Tower lit up.

He slid the ring onto her finger, then stood up and drew her to her feet. 'So we're officially engaged.'

She remembered what he'd said, the night she'd proposed to him: he'd wait for her until they got engaged.

Suddenly there wasn't enough air—which was ridiculous, considering they were outside.

'We need a selfie for the parents,' she said, suddenly panicking.

'You have a point. And we have about four minutes to get a good shot.' He stood behind her with his arms round her, and she held her left hand up, displaying the ring.

He held his phone out. 'Smile—three, two, one…' He snapped the photograph of them together, with the Eiffel Tower sparkling in the background. 'And now just the hands.' He slid one hand under hers and she curled her fingers round his hand, displaying the ring.

'Perfect,' he said, and spun her round so he could kiss her. 'We'll send this to your parents, mine, and Darcy, later tonight. But first I want to dance with my new fiancée.' He flicked into his music app, and she recognised the song immediately: George Michael's version of 'The First Time Ever I Saw Your Face'.

'It's a song that was written way before both of us were born,' he said. 'But it says every-thing I want to say to you. I love you, Fizz.'

'I love you, too, Oli,' she said. She stepped

into his arms, closed her eyes, and as they began to dance she kissed him.

She wasn't sure which of them moved off the terrace first, or which of them closed the door and the curtains behind them. But then he'd swept her off her feet and was carrying her to that beautiful wide bed.

And, as he set her back on her feet, seven years of waiting was finally over.

EPILOGUE

One year later

DARCY ADJUSTED FIZZ'S veil when she'd climbed out of the car and handed her bouquet to her, ready for the photographer to take the traditional photographs of the bride, the matron of honour and their father.

The empire line wedding dress covered her bump—the little bit of news that Fizz and Oliver weren't quite ready to share with their family, until Fizz had reached the twelve-week point and stopped worrying quite so much.

Darcy smiled. 'You look amazing.'

'So do you.' Darcy was also wearing an empire line dress, except hers was in sapphire blue rather than ivory, and there were small sunflowers threaded into her updo to go with the sunflowers in Fizz's bouquet.

'The sun's out,' their father remarked. 'And it's warm for December.'

'That's our Laura making sure my hair stays nice until after the photos are done,' Fizz said. 'I think she'd be pleased with the result of her bucket list.' She looked at Darcy. 'You married to Arturo, me about to marry Oli—both of us settled and happy, the way she wanted us to be.' Fizz and Oliver had sold their flats and had moved into a terraced house in Chalk Farm, the previous month; Tilly the cat had settled happily into her new abode, either people-watching from the back of the sofa in the living room, or curled on a cushion next to Fizz in her workroom.

'She would,' Darcy agreed. 'She'd have loved Ruby and Tilly, too. And she'd be pleased that you chose her favourite flower for your theme. That cake your friend made with the cascade of sunflowers down it is *incredible!*'

Fizz blinked back the prick of tears. She'd always miss Laura—always—but today was a day for smiles. The day that she and Oliver pledged their love in front of their family and friends.

'Ready to go, love?' her father asked. 'Or do you want to be traditionally late?'

Fizz smiled. 'I think I've kept Oli waiting for long enough.'

'Agreed.' Darcy laughed, and made a last adjustment to Fizz's veil. 'All set.'

'All set,' Fizz said, and her father pushed the church door fully open.

Oliver heard the creaking of the church door as he stood at the altar. Then the usher had clearly alerted the organist, who started to play Pachelbel's Canon. And Oliver found his pulse rate rocketing at the idea of his bride walking down the altar to him.

Sanjay, his best man, nudged him. 'You can look now. Actually, you should *definitely* look. She's the definition of a radiant bride.'

Oliver turned round, and he couldn't help smiling as the woman he loved walked down the aisle of the Victorian church towards him, carrying a bouquet of sunflowers softened with gypsophila, holding on to her father's arm and with Darcy bringing up the rear.

I love you, he mouthed as Fizz handed her bouquet to Darcy and came to stand beside him.

Love you, too, she mouthed back.

Everything was perfect. The music, the weather, the smiles on all the guests' faces. Fizz's father reading from Corinthians about love being patient, and the mischief on Fizz's face when she squeezed his fingers and mouthed, *You were beyond patient. Seven years!*

His mother reading Shakespeare's *Sonnet 116.*

The vicar asking if Felicity Bennett would take Oliver Harrison as her lawful wedded husband, and the love in her eyes as she said, 'I will.'

The two of them exchanging the rings she'd made, simple bands of gold engraved inside with their initials and the date.

The vicar declaring them man and wife, and finally the words he'd been looking forward to: 'You may kiss the bride.'

Maybe he lingered a little too much over the kiss, because their guests all cheered, and when he broke the kiss Fizz was laughing.

The guests showered them with delphinium petals as they left the church; he helped Fizz into the old-fashioned Rolls-Royce, then climbed in beside her. They posed for a couple of photographs before Sanjay closed the car door, and the Rolls-Royce drove slowly down the gravelled track.

'Well, Mrs Bennett-Harrison.' He savoured the words.

'Indeed, Mr Bennett-Harrison,' she said with a grin.

'Ready to start the rest of our lives?' he asked.

'Now and for always,' she said.

And this time he took his time kissing his new bride, all the way to the gorgeous Queen Anne building just down the road in Hampstead, which housed an art gallery and music room where they were holding the reception.

Once they'd greeted their guests and made sure that everyone had a glass of passionfruit martini or champagne in the music room, the wedding breakfast was served in the art gallery section of the house. The tables were in a horseshoe shape, covered with starched white tablecloths, and the arrangements of tiny sunflowers brought a touch of extra brightness to the room.

'Trust you to hold your reception in an art gallery,' Darcy teased.

'I was an art student and my new husband's a fine art dealer. Of course we'd celebrate in an art gallery,' Fizz answered with a grin.

Oliver chuckled. 'We did think about hiring the middle of the Eiffel Tower.'

'Except dancing isn't allowed on their glass

floor. So that's a no. Because this is a party,'
Fizz said, 'and I want dancing.'

Darcy smiled. 'I'm not scared of dancing
any more. Thanks to Arturo.'

'Good. Because you're dancing with me,
later. All of you.' Fizz hugged her brother-
in-law.

The food was wonderful—a wild mushroom and thyme tart garnished with edible
petals, chicken marinaded in lime and served
with sweet potato mash and green beans, and
a *café gourmand* at Fizz's special request with
a mini crème brûlée, lemon curd tart and a
blueberry Eton mess. Fizz had also arranged
a special bottle for herself, which looked like
champagne from the outside but was actually
sparkling elderflower, and the bar staff had
all been quietly briefed that if anyone bought
Fizz a cocktail they should mix her a special
version of a passionfruit martini without the
vodka and with sparkling water in place of
prosecco.

After the meal, everyone's drinks were
topped up and Fizz's dad made a short but
very sweet speech, Sanjay enjoyed telling terrible stories about Oliver's student days.

And then it was Oliver's turn.

'I think everyone knows I fell in love with

Fizz the very day I met her, but it was never the right time to tell her—until she had to do Laura's bucket list, and asked me to go to Paris with her.' He bent down to steal a kiss from his new bride. 'Maybe if I'd taken her there years ago, we wouldn't have wasted all that time being just best friends. Maybe I'm just a bit slow on the uptake. Or maybe she would've turned me down and this year was exactly the right time for me to tell her how I really felt about her.' He smiled. 'And now I'm going to shut up. Thank you all for coming to celebrate with us, but most of all thank you to Fizz for marrying me and making me the happiest man in the universe.' He raised his glass. 'I give you my bride. It's taken me seven years to get her to the altar, but she's worth the wait. Fizz Bennett-Harrison.'

'Fizz,' everyone echoed, raising their glasses.

And then it was time to go into the music room, with its gorgeous light wood panelling and elegant sconces. A baby grand piano was installed at one end, flanked by enormous ferns; they'd hired a pianist and singer to perform a mixture of songs, from slow jazz-based numbers through to dance-floor fillers, so there was something for everyone for their guests.

But the first dance was theirs alone.

And, after Paris, there was only one song it could be.

Oliver looked at Fizz as the first notes of 'The First Time Ever I Saw Your Face' floated into the room. She smiled, slipped into his arms, and began to waltz with him.

Halfway through, their parents, Darcy and Arturo, and Sanjay and his partner Ruby joined them on the dance floor.

'Happy?' Oliver asked, looking into Fizz's eyes.

She smiled. 'With you? Always.'

* * * * *

If you missed the previous story in
The Life-Changing List duet,
then check out
Slow Dance with the Italian
by Scarlet Wilson

And if you enjoyed this story,
check out these other great reads
from Kate Hardy

Wedding Deal with Her Rival
Tempted by Her Fake Fiancé
Crowning His Secret Princess

All available now!